PERFECTED SINFULNESS

Michael J. Gilbert

ISBN: 0615896715
ISBN-13: 9780615896717
Library of Congress Control Number: 2013919758
Sisyphus's Joy, Monticello, IN

The social impulse is, in the first place, negatively defined by the law of absolute harmony;—it must not contradict itself. The impulse leads to reciprocal activity, to mutual influence, mutual giving and receiving, mutual suffering and doing,—not to mere causality—not to mere activity, of which others are but the passive objects.

—Johann Gottlieb Fichte

Smile and others will smile back. Smile to show how transparent, how candid you are. Smile if you have nothing to say. Most of all, do not hide the fact you have nothing to say nor your total indifference to others. Let this emptiness, this profound indifference shine out spontaneously in your smile.

—Jean Baudrillard

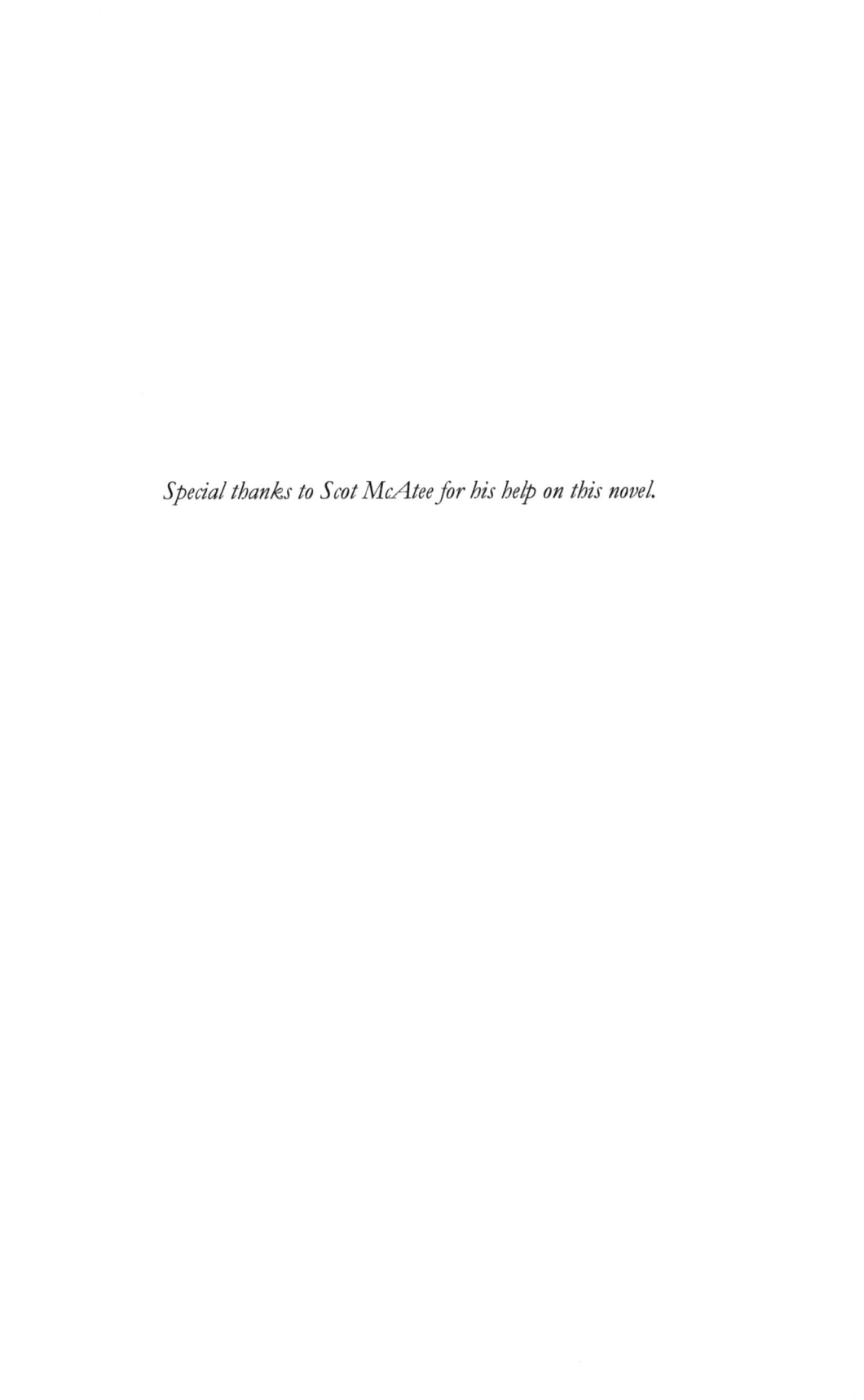

Special thanks to Scot McAtee for his help on this novel.

CHAPTER ONE
It Just So Happens

Franki Rose

"It's him. It's really him!" I exclaim before I regain my composure.

"Who?" Ryah asks as she looks up from her menu.

"Elijah Noor. That has to be him. My God, I haven't seen him in years."

"Who's Elijah Noor?" Ryah asks. I notice her checking him out, and for some reason it angers me.

"I grew up with him. We went to the same high school. I can't believe it's him. I haven't seen him since we graduated ten years ago."

Ryah is staring at him. "Did you date him?" She flips her hair after asking the question.

"No, I would've told you if I had. I always had a crush on him, though," I confess.

"I think I vaguely remember you mentioning him." Ryah squeezes a lemon slice into her glass of water. "You're way too passive, Franki," she blurts. "How do you expect to ever get what you want if you don't take it?" Ryah's eyes remain fixed on Eli as she licks the lemon juice from her fingertips.

"I was shy back then."

"And what is your excuse now?" Ryah asks casually.

"What do you mean?"

"I mean, why are you still sitting here? Go over there and say hello." Ryah sips water through her straw and looks at me with the same devious expression she used in high school after she dared me to do something she knew would make me feel uncomfortable.

"I could never do that."

"And why not?" she persists. I look at Eli again. His straight black hair is longer than I remember him keeping it. He has leaned down a bit, maybe too much, but as he turns to look toward the street I can see his unmistakable soft facial features. I could recognize that baby face anywhere.

"I don't want to disturb him."

"Disturb him? He's sitting alone. Get up and go over there. He'll be happy to see you," Ryah urges.

"Do you think so?"

"Absolutely." Ryah's impatience is evident. I look at Eli. "Quit worrying and go!" Ryah orders. I feel anxious. *What do I say?* I can sense the force of my pulse in my neck. I try to calm myself with a deep breath. I wish it wasn't so difficult to talk to people.

I lean forward in my chair. "Do you really think I should go? He hasn't seen me since high school. What if he doesn't remember me? Even worse, what if he doesn't want to talk to me?"

"Go," is all she says in a curt tone.

I clear my throat and stand up. I approach him as I try to think of something to say. Nothing comes to mind. Suddenly I'm standing behind him. "Eli, is that you?" I say as I feign surprise. He looks over his shoulder at me and then perks up as he smiles.

"Franki Rose?" he asks, and then before I can respond, "How in the hell are you?" He stands and hugs me. He smells like expensive cologne.

"I'm well. How are you? God, it's been forever." After I speak, he looks at me for a moment without saying anything. Only the outlines of his eyes are visible behind his black sunglasses. I am exposed and it terrifies me.

"I'm well," he replies after an extended pause. "I'm sorry. Wow, I can't believe it's you. How long has it been?" he asks.

"Since high school."

"That seems like so long ago." His attention remains focused on me. I blush.

"What have you been up to?" I ask in an attempt to deter his attention from my reddening face.

"Where do I begin? Do you remember when I went off to college and had no idea what I wanted to do with my life?"

I laugh innocently. "Yes, I remember."

"Well, I majored in political science. I graduated and still had no idea what I wanted to do, so I went to law school. I graduated a few years ago, and now I'm right back where I started."

"What brought you back here? You always used to say that when you left you'd never come back." He's wearing a designer blazer, and his button-up shirt is freshly pressed. He never used to dress so nicely. I wish I could see his eyes.

"My father isn't doing so well," he says in a flat tone.

"I'm sorry to hear that. I didn't know."

"It's not your fault. He had a heart attack about a year ago. When he couldn't maintain his usual work schedule, he asked me if I would come home and help him run the restaurant. So now I'm back in town managing the business until he starts feeling better." Eli looks down for a moment. I can tell he is upset.

"Is your father doing better?" I ask, not knowing what to say.

"He's healing slowly. You know how he is, though. He constantly bitches about his diet and exercise program. I swear the old man will never relax and enjoy life. Here, have a seat." Eli motions to the chair across from him, urging me to sit.

"Oh, I can't stay. I'm here with my girlfriend." I turn and point in Ryah's direction. She's looking at both of us coyly and offers a delicate wave. *Did she wave at me or Eli?*

"Pardon me. I didn't mean to sound presumptuous. I thought you might be here alone. I can allow you to get back to your friend," he says while still looking at Ryah. I feel jealous that he's eyeing Ryah, but I act like it doesn't bother me.

"Don't be silly. She can wait. I haven't seen you in so long." I cringe once I realize how pathetic I must sound. *Did I just repeat what I said earlier?* I don't want him to think I'm too interested.

"We'll have to get coffee sometime and catch up if you're free." His full attention is directed toward me again.

"I would love that," I say. I can't stop myself from smiling. I've never been good at disguising my feelings.

"OK, let me get your number." Eli takes his phone from the inside pocket of his blazer. He types my number into his phone as I recite it.

"I'll have to come by the restaurant. I can't imagine you working at Wayside. Didn't your father fire you from the restaurant when you were in high school?" I joke.

Eli smirks. "Yes, he did. Now he needs me, so he's a little more patient," Eli says while still grinning.

"I don't know about you, Eli. But hey, I better get back to Ryah. I'll plan to see you soon." I find myself unable to move. I always fail to leave when I should.

"You know where to find me, Franki. No matter how many years have passed, some things never change. I always find it strange how life has a way of coming full circle."

CHAPTER TWO

I Shouldn't

Ryah Klein

"**Y**ou have to go," I repeat to Kasey, who is still breathing heavily. I see the sweat on his bare chest. He looks good.

"Why, Ryah? Do you have somewhere else to be?" he asks in a playful manner. I'm in no mood to entertain Kasey. I thought he was hot when he was unavailable, but now I think he's annoying.

"Actually I do have somewhere to be," I reply as I gather my clothes and start to dress. I look at him again. He has a big dopey grin on his face. I can't stand to look at him. I utter an audible sigh and leave the bedroom.

"Come on. Why are you being like this?" I hear him yell from the bedroom where I left him. I get dressed while standing in the living room. As I slide my jeans on, I look out my front window overlooking Merrin Street at the people passing by on the sidewalk. I recognize almost all of them. God, I hate small towns.

"Did I do something wrong?" Kasey asks as he enters the living room. He buttons his jeans and pauses as he waits for me to respond. "Ryah—" he begins before I cut him off.

"You didn't do anything," I assure him. "I just have a lot on my mind." I feel the beaming sunlight on my skin. I close my eyes and savor the warmth. For a second, I forget Kasey is here.

"Are you all right?" I hear Kasey ask. I open my eyes.

"Don't worry about it, OK. I don't need to talk about every damn detail of my life. We're not together. You know that, right?" I say harshly without any remorse. I loathe myself for ever desiring Kasey.

"I know," he replies sheepishly. I can tell I hurt his feelings but I can't make myself care. I watch him finish getting dressed as I button my black lace blouse. He keeps looking at me. I stare back at him. I tire of the game and look out the window again. I can hear his movements stop. Then the floor creaks. I turn around just as he's approaching.

"Can I call you later?" His question sounds more like an apology.

I look at him without blinking. "I don't think that would be a good idea," I say dispassionately. "I'll call you." I am willing to say anything to get him to leave.

"OK." He takes a step toward me. I turn away from him. I hear him walk toward the door. Then I hear the door open and close.

I watch Kasey from my living room window as he walks toward his car. He pauses on the sidewalk and looks up at me. I don't know if he can see me or not. I stare down at him. His face looks pained. He gets into his car. I don't know why he is so weak.

As Kasey drives away, I scramble to finish getting dressed. I put my diamond stud earrings in my ears and check my hair in the mirror. My face is still a bit flushed. I always feel like I am glowing after sex. The pleasure stays with me for hours. I run both hands through my hair and close my eyes as I take a deep breath. I open my eyes and study my reflection in the mirror as I smile.

***

I know I shouldn't visit him. It will harm Franki. I know this, but I still go. I walk into Wayside and stroll through the dining area of the restaurant to the bar, which is in a separate room toward the back of the building. As I approach the bar, I slow my walk and take more deliberate steps. I see Eli immediately. He is even more attractive than I remember. His straight black hair hangs haphazardly just over his collar. His shirt is unbuttoned just enough to reveal his tan skin, which contrasts nicely with his yellow shirt. He sees me and stops mixing the drink he holds in his hand. I smile and sit on the barstool directly in front of him. He smiles back at me before he resumes mixing the drink.

"I'll be right with you, miss," he says. I don't offer a response. There are only ten or so people here, which I guess is an average crowd for a Tuesday evening in late August. I try to act like I'm watching the television on the wall but quickly lose interest once I realize a baseball game is on.

"I'm sorry about your wait," he says as he approaches. I try to look casual, but I can feel my heart beating in my chest. "What can I get you?"

"I'll have a sangria." Our eyes meet. I grin and then cover my mouth to appear shy, even though I'm not.

"Coming right up," he says without diverting his eyes from mine.

"Thank you," I reply in a soft but flirtatious voice. I watch him as he selects a glass and pours the drink. His jeans are dark blue and tight enough that I can see his athletic physique. I admire his ass until he turns around and almost catches me looking.

"Pardon me for asking," he says as he places the drink in front of me, "but have I met you before? You look familiar, but I can't place you."

"Do you ask that question to every female who orders a drink?" I tease.

He clears his throat. "No. I'm serious. I swear I've seen you before."

"Is that so?" I take a drink.

"Maybe I'm mistaken."

"I'm Franki's friend," I admit.

"Oh, that's right. The patio…I saw you with Franki this past Sunday."

"Yeah. How could you forget?"

"You'll have to forgive me. I've been a bit distracted since I moved back here."

"I guess everyone is allowed one mistake." I take another drink.

He wipes the bar with a towel and then stops. "I'm Elijah Noor, by the way." His eyes are greenish brown.

"Nice to meet you, Elijah. I'm Ryah Klein. You better not forget me a second time."

He smiles and looks away. "I promise I won't forget you." I watch his lips move as he speaks.

"I'm not worried," I say. "I'll make sure you remember me."

CHAPTER THREE
Childhood Friends

Elijah Noor

I tend to destroy others. I don't know why, but I do. It will happen again, I'm sure. It has only been two years since I graduated from law school. Now I find myself back in my hometown fraternizing with the same people I vowed I would never speak to after I left. It had never been my goal to be a lawyer. In fact, I never really wanted to do anything. I'm often bored. I find the things that interest most people to be completely absurd. I don't portray myself as someone who is disengaged, though. I guess I've always been way too concerned with how people perceive me to rebel openly. That's my real problem. I can't be myself because I don't want people to know who I really am. I've only ever been hurt by people who claimed that they loved me. Based on my past, I don't think wanting to hide certain parts of myself is abnormal. It's absolutely necessary to avoid being harmed by others. Plus, life would be unbearable if people saw us as we truly are. Sometimes life doesn't make any sense.

I watch her walk out of the bar. I can't help that she visited me. I wonder if Franki suspects her friend would do such a thing. I doubt that she does. People want to trust others. It provides a false sense of hope that people are innately good. I pour myself a glass of water and drink it slowly. I notice the half-smoked cigarette Ryah left in the ashtray. The smoke curls as it hangs in the air. I look around at the few remaining patrons and realize not much has changed since I left Payne, Ohio, ten years ago.

Bo Schnep walks into the bar and immediately does a double take.

"Eli…damn, it is you. I haven't seen you in years," he says while extending his hand to shake mine. I shake his hand dutifully and then wipe my palm with the towel draped over my shoulder. "How have you been?"

"I've been well. How about yourself?" I ask, even though I don't care. I have despised Bo Schnep ever since the fifth grade, when I caught him kissing Emily Grant. The whole week before the incident, Bo kept asking me during our walk to school who I liked the most in our grade. I finally confided to Bo that I liked Emily the most. I trusted him. The very next day I caught him kissing her in the gym after school. He never knew I saw him. Later I made Emily cry when I called her an ugly whore in front of Bo at the park. I could tell Bo wanted to console her, but he didn't. She kept staring at him while she cried. I sometimes think of that day. Ever since that moment, I have felt a burning hatred for Bo. I always imagined I would get even, but I've been patient. I want it to sting him badly. I want it to destroy his core. He will never see it coming.

"Not much has changed here. I made detective on the force two years ago, so that's been keeping me pretty busy."

I imagine he still believes we're friends. I feel a rage building as I look into his eyes. His good looks conceal a stupid acceptance of everything visible.

"That's great," I say with forced excitement. "It's nice to know that talent gets rewarded." I almost gag as I speak. It's so contrived.

"I appreciate it, Eli. What are you doing back in Payne? I thought you were off to conquer the world." Bo appears sincerely interested.

"My father had a heart attack. I decided that I would postpone a career in law and return home to help with the restaurant until his health improves," I say as I place a coaster on the bar in front of Bo. "Are you drinking?" I ask.

"Sure. I'll have a draft beer. I'd like to buy you one too," he offers.

"That is awful kind of you," I reply as I grab two glasses and fill them with beer. I place his beer in front of him.

"A toast to friends being reunited," Bo says as he raises his glass. I raise mine too, and we both take a drink. "I sure am glad I came in here tonight," he says.

I smile. "It's nice to see a friendly face. I've missed this town." I've learned that sometimes a smile represents the greatest form of deceit.

CHAPTER FOUR

Taking a Chance

Franki Rose

"**D**o you need anything else?" I ask the middle-aged couple. They say that they are fine. I turn around to check on my only other occupied table when I see Eli approaching the coffee shop. I act like I don't see him. I walk to the next table. Old man Gunther asks for a refill. I go to retrieve the coffee pot and take a moment to glance at my reflection in the glass of the door as I leave the patio. My hair looks hideous. My ponytail is not styled and my brown hair looks flat. To make matters even worse, my legs feel sweaty. I wish I would have worn nicer shorts. I didn't think I would see anyone but the usual Saturday morning customers. Eli sits at a table far from the other customers. He is wearing sunglasses. His black V-neck T-shirt fits him nicely and matches his dark-blue jeans perfectly. His boots look casual but expensive. I don't want him to see me.

I approach Ed Gunther on the patio and fill his mug with coffee. "Is there anything else?" I ask. He shakes his head without taking his eyes from his newspaper. Eli is sitting so that he is facing the street. A couple walks past the café with a tiny dog on a leash. A man in a suit waits at a crosswalk.

Eli sees me walking toward his table and smiles. "Hello, Franki," he says in a casual tone. He looks so attractive I need a brief moment to gather myself before responding.

"Eli, what are you doing here?" I ask. I hate myself for sounding so girlish.

"I was told this is where I could find you. Since you haven't visited me at Wayside, I thought I would surprise you."

"How kind of you. Now you know where I work," I say, trying to fight the embarrassment I feel.

"I do. Why haven't you made an appearance at Wayside?" he asks.

"I guess I've been busy," I say. I'm impressed that he wants to see me. My hands are clammy. "Can I get you something to drink?" I ask.

"I'll have a Diet Coke," he replies.

"No problem. I'll be right back." I leave the patio area to get his drink. Once I'm inside the store, I take a deep breath. I watch Eli through the store window. He reclines in his chair and takes out his cell phone. He appears to send a text and then places his phone on the table in front of him. I pour his drink and walk back out to the patio.

"Here you go, Eli. Can I get you anything else?" I place a straw in front of him after I ask. He slowly peels away the paper wrapper and places the straw in his drink. Two sparrows land on the sidewalk directly in front of us and then fly away, with one in pursuit of the other.

"I would like for you to sit with me."

His confidence turns me on. I clear my throat. "I don't think my boss would appreciate that."

"Your other customers don't appear to need anything at the moment." He motions his hand to offer me a seat next to him.

I want to sit down so badly, but I don't want to appear too eager. "I suppose I can sit for a minute and talk to an old friend."

He smiles and helps move the chair so that I can sit down. "That's more like it." I feel awkward sitting next to Eli. My company polo shirt is clinging to my back and feels gross against my skin. I can only imagine how horrible I look to him, although he doesn't offer any indication that my worry is warranted.

"So…Franki Rose…" he begins as he turns his chair so he can look at me without turning his head.

"Eli Noor…"

"Are you married?" he asks abruptly. "The last time I visited, you had been in a serious relationship for a few years."

"I'm not married. I was with Kasey Price for almost three years, but we broke up a few months ago."

"I'm sorry to hear that," he says in a sincere voice.

"Don't be," I reveal. "It's for the better. He's a great guy. It just didn't work out."

"Did you two grow apart? I hate when that happens. It's crazy to me how people gradually change until one day they are unrecognizable to even those who once knew them so well." Eli turns his head as if he's reflecting on his statement.

"It was mainly a trust issue," I disclose. "I couldn't trust him."

"Trust is dangerous," he says.

"I agree. I suspected he had a thing for my friend Ryah, but I couldn't prove it, and he certainly wouldn't admit anything to me."

"That's a shame. Did Ryah suspect that he was interested in her?" he asks. I fear that I'm boring him with small-town drama.

"She promised me that he had never said or done anything inappropriate. I believe her. She's been my best friend since high school. It didn't matter, though. I didn't feel like he was being totally honest with me, and I guess my insecurities finally caused me to break it off with him."

"People frighten me," Eli declares before he looks away from me and directs his attention toward the street. A couple of children in a neighboring yard scream playfully as they squirt each other with water guns.

"You shouldn't be frightened by people. Relationships make us better. Caring about someone more than you care about yourself is what makes this life livable."

"Is that possible? I mean, do you actually believe that?" he asks as he turns his head to face me again.

"I have to."

CHAPTER FIVE
She's Too Nice

Elijah Noor

I don't know why I am here. I guess I feel obligated, for whatever reason. I watch Franki talk with a couple at a neighboring table. She smiles frequently and doesn't at all appear rushed. She takes time to listen to the customers before she leaves their table. She walks inside the coffee shop and after a few minutes emerges with to-go cups and their bill. The couple pays her and she thanks them graciously before walking back inside the shop. I can't help thinking that I shouldn't have come.

An elderly woman enters the patio and sits by herself at a corner table. I study Franki as she greets the woman. Franki stands patiently as the woman talks incessantly about something that happened to her a day ago. I quit listening and sip my Diet Coke. I keep thinking about Ryah Klein. She intrigues me for some reason. Maybe it's because I know she is bad. I like the way her dark-brown hair always looks tousled. Those blue eyes are impossible to forget. Her slender figure makes her look younger than she is. I can't remember her from high school. I think she attended a neighboring school, but I'm not sure. All I know is that there's something more to her.

It's never easy to disappoint people. I don't ever intend to do so, but it invariably happens. An incoming text message reads, "What are you doing?" I don't have the number saved in my phone, but I recognize the area code as local.

"Who is this?" I text back.

"Guess," the next text I receive says. I set my phone down and take a drink. I listen to the faint music playing from the coffee shop speakers. I can't believe I will be twenty-eight in three months. A few minutes pass. I lift my phone from the table and send a text that says, "I give up."

I feel an adrenaline rush when I read the next text message that simply says, "Ryah."

"Do you have to work tonight?" I hear a voice ask. I slide my phone in the front pocket of my jeans and look up to see Franki standing beside me. I hope she didn't see my phone's screen. I act as if she didn't.

"I do," I say while settling myself. My mouth feels dry so I take a drink.

"Oh, OK."

"Why?" I ask.

"I don't know. I thought maybe we could get a drink." I can tell after Franki speaks that she is nervous.

"I would like that." Franki smiles. "How about I call you and we'll go out next week," I offer.

"That would be wonderful." She turns to walk away until I stop her.

"Franki," I say in a louder voice to get her attention.

"Yes?" She stops and turns to face me. She looks adorable.

"I'm glad I visited you today."

"So am I," she utters.

"I'll see you soon," I promise. Franki smiles and kind of shrugs her shoulders involuntarily as if she can't contain her excitement before turning around and walking away.

I wait until Franki is busy with another table before I take my phone from my pocket and check for another text from Ryah. I discover one unread text message and open it. It reads, "What are you doing?" I start to type a reply and then stop. I look up and see Franki still talking with the elderly woman. Franki and the woman laugh, and the old woman pats Franki's arm. Franki catches me watching her. I don't look away. She is a good person.

CHAPTER SIX

What a Bore

Ryah Klein

He parks his car on Merrin Street. I watch him from my bedroom window as he approaches my building. He appears eager. It's a little after seven in the evening. A group of young children ride their bicycles up and down the sidewalk. Two teenagers sneak a smoke in an alleyway. The anticipation is what makes this so exciting. I admit it. I like it when he says he needs me, but that's not enough. There has to be something more. I hear a knock at the front door and take a deep breath.

"How are you, Ryah? Damn, you look amazing." The words rush from his mouth. I look him up and down without answering and then move to the side so he can enter my apartment. Bo is wearing a black single-breasted suit with a white oxford dress shirt and a matching black tie with a full Windsor knot. His blond hair is styled with product and is even more curly than usual. He is tan and handsome. I hug him and feel his fingertips dig into the small of my back. His heart beats against my chest as he holds me. I break from his embrace and look up at him. Bo's breathing is irregular. He is all mine for as long as I want him.

"I have to be back—" he begins before I cut him off.

"I know. I don't want to hear any excuses why you can't stay."

"It's not that—" he tries to continue.

"Don't say anything." I take his hand and guide him to my bedroom. The bed is bare except for the sheets, which are freshly laundered. A lit candle by the window gives off a strong aroma of blueberries. I turn him so that his back is facing my bed. I give him a gentle kiss on the lips but pull back as soon as he tries to kiss me back. I look at him. I can tell he wants to say something, but he doesn't. I push him with just enough force that he falls backward. He is sitting on the edge of my bed. He looks confused.

I slide my tank top off with one fluid motion while standing in front of Bo. He shifts his position on the bed a bit. I stand in front of him with my breasts bared. He attempts to stand but stops when I put my hand on his shoulder. I remove my hand from his shoulder once he is still and undo my jeans. I pull them down slowly until I am standing in front of him in only my pink lace panties. He's sweating. He stares at me without blinking. His desire turns me on. I pull my dark-brown hair back off my neck and bunch it up on the top of my head before I let it go. It cascades down my back. He tries to stand again. I push him back with my hand, but this time he resists and brushes my hand away. I take a step back as he stands. He seizes me. I can feel his muscular arms wrap around my waist as his mouth touches mine.

***

Bo lies next to me as I stare at the torn condom wrapper on the floor. I feel his hand on my back, but it doesn't comfort me. I don't care about Bo, and I don't think he cares about me. It's just sex. I roll over and notice that the flower in the vase on my windowsill needs water.

"Ryah, I've got to go soon," Bo finally says after he kisses my shoulder.

"What time does the police banquet start?"

"Nine."

"Who are you going with?" I turn over in bed and look at him as he stares at the ceiling.

"I'm going with a friend." I don't believe Bo, but I don't really care if he's being dishonest, so I don't argue.

"What do you do at those silly things?"

He kisses my forehead. "It's mostly used to acknowledge years of service, promotions, and a few yearly awards. It's nothing big."

"Do you get a decent meal?" I don't know why I'm asking questions, because I am not at all interested in Bo's answers.

"It's OK. The Eckerle family, who runs the bed-and-breakfast, caters the event. The roast beef is good."

"That does sound good," I say. I hear him take a deep breath, then he kisses my cheek and gets out of bed. I watch him walk out of the bedroom and hear him turn the shower on. I listen to the water going down the drain as I light a cigarette. I blow the smoke toward the ceiling. His shower is brief, and he returns with a towel wrapped around his waist. He made sure not to wet his hair. I lie on my side and watch as he gets dressed. Bo is always so particular about his attire. He takes time to smooth out any wrinkles in his shirt and then makes sure the shirt is tucked into his black pants perfectly. He tightens his tie and inspects the knot while looking in the mirror that rests on top of my dresser. I don't want to resist my attraction to Bo.

"Can I see you again?" he asks while sitting on the edge of the bed and leaning down to kiss my lips.

"That's a possibility." I pull him to me and kiss him again.

"I need to," he confesses. His hand cups my right breast. I feel my body tingle.

"I like it when you need me."

"I know you do. I can't help it, Ryah. You're so good to me."

"I'm your best-kept secret." I can tell the comment upsets him. He can't figure me out, and that frustrates him. I enjoy it when men try to understand me. It makes me feel powerful, like I can control their every thought.

"Don't say that," he says.

"Why not? It's the truth."

"No, it isn't. Tell me you don't really believe that, Ryah."

"Why wouldn't I believe that?"

"Because it's not true."

"If you say so."

"Are you upset?"

"Not at all." I roll over so that my back is facing him.

He groans. "Ryah, don't be like this."

"I'm not being like anything."

"I have to go."

"Bye."

"Can I call you tomorrow?"

I brush my hair off my face with my left hand. "You can try."

"Please?"

"You better leave, Bo. I don't want you to keep your date waiting." I feel the bed shift as he stands up. I sense him peering down at me, but I don't turn to face him. He starts to say something but stops. I hear his footsteps leave the bedroom and then hear my front door open and close. I roll over, feeling satisfied.

CHAPTER SEVEN
Police Banquet

Scarlett Davison

He's late. I walk to the window and then back to the kitchen table, where I check my phone even though it hasn't sounded with an incoming message. I pour myself a glass of water and take a drink. I don't know why I agreed to go to the damn banquet in the first place. I guess I have been feeling lonely. It has been almost two years since the breakup that changed everything. I want to matter to someone. I haven't felt pretty in a long time. I check my phone again.

I never should have returned to Payne. I guess I thought a familiar setting would allow me to heal. I wanted something safe. I still hope that some part of me can be recovered. I have to believe that somehow life matters, even when it feels like it doesn't. There has to be a reason for all of the pain. *Where is he?*

I hear his car pull into the driveway. I stand at the door and open it just as he attempts to knock.

"I'm sorry," is what he says as soon as he sees me. "I tried—" he begins.

"Let's go."

"I'm sorry," he repeats.

As my anger subsides, I look over at him while we're in his car and appreciate how handsome he looks in his black suit. I lean back in my seat and enjoy the stream of cool air blowing against my bare legs from the air-conditioning vents. When we arrive, Bo parks near the back of the parking lot, but before he gets out of the car, he turns to me and says, "I really am sorry, Scarlett. I didn't mean to be late. Will you forgive me?"

"I'm over it," I say as I turn to face him. "Let's try to enjoy the evening."

"I agree. Next time I'll call you if I'm running late. I was sure I would make it on time. I'm not sure what's wrong with my cell phone. It's not holding a charge lately. It won't happen again." I don't really believe Bo's claim, but I don't care enough to exert energy trying to argue.

Bo introduces me to a variety of people as we make our way to our assigned table. I don't remember many of their names, but the gesture is nice.

"Do you know any of these people?" he asks.

"I don't. It's been years since I've spent any time in Payne. I tried like hell to avoid this place." Bo takes a drink of water and then offers to pour me some wine. I provide my glass and indicate I would prefer the Chardonnay.

"So what brought you back?"

"I don't know. I guess I couldn't get over my past." Just as I finish talking, some guy named Dan comes over and shakes Bo's hand. They share a laugh. Dan pats Bo on the back and leaves. I don't think Bo even listened to my answer.

The meal is good. I drink another glass of wine after finishing my entrée, even though I shouldn't. Person after person passes by our table and greets Bo. When Bo introduces me, I smile and wave politely. I think about how everything was different before I lost my belief in love. I can't stop thinking about the times I shared with my ex in the tiny house we rented on Vine Street. I miss the way he used to caress my back in the mornings. I can almost feel his fingertips pressed against my skin. I want those times back. I want to laugh with him. I want his arms wrapped around me. I wish I could relive the moment we shared in the bathtub the first night we moved in together. I smile while thinking of the way he sang "Itsy Bitsy Spider" as his fingers moved up my leg until they touched me and I felt the breath leave my lungs. I cover my mouth to conceal a giggle, which escapes as I remember me jumping in the pile of leaves he raked in our front yard that fall. He grabbed me right after and told me he would never let me go. That all changed when…

"Scarlett, I want you to meet Charlie." As I look up to see who Bo is introducing, I immediately recognize the face.

"Hello, Scarlett."

"How are you, Charlie?"

"You two know each other?" Bo asks.

"Yes. We—"

"I knew Scarlett years ago, before she moved away," Charlie discloses.

"Oh, great," Bo says.

"It's nice to see you, Charlie. It has been a long time."

"Yes, it has."

Charlie stares at me for a moment as if he is trying to figure something out. I finish my wine. "Well, I better get back to Terra. It was really great seeing you two." Bo shakes Charlie's hand before he leaves our table.

Once Charlie is a distance away from us, Bo turns to me as I am pouring another glass of wine.

"Did you two go to school together?"

I take a drink of wine. "No."

"How do you know him?" Bo asks.

"It's a long story."

"Oh."

I can tell Bo is worried for some reason. "He was a friend of a friend. Can we leave soon?"

CHAPTER EIGHT
A Night to Remember

Franki Rose

I hear a knock at the door and take one more look at myself in the mirror. I open the door. Eli is standing in the doorway wearing a blue button-up shirt that is undone just enough that I can tell he isn't wearing an undershirt. His skin looks especially tan as he stands in the darkness. I notice his pressed dark-blue jeans. His black boots complement his outfit nicely. He is holding a single yellow daisy in his right hand. Eli extends the flower to me. I smile.

"You look amazing," he says with such sincerity that I feel chills.

I accept the flower from him. "How did you know daisies are my favorite flower?"

"How could I forget? You used to draw them on all of your notebooks in middle school."

"Wow. I can't believe you remember that. I'm embarrassed."

"Don't be. It's adorable."

I can't stop smiling. "Come in while I get a vase. You don't understand how much I love daisies. They make me so happy."

"Every beautiful woman deserves a flower," he says as he steps inside my apartment. "I would prefer you didn't put it in a vase, though."

I stop in the entranceway of the kitchen. "What do you mean?" I ask as I turn around.

"I would rather you wear it."

"Wear it? How? I mean, where would I put it?"

"Oh, Franki…do you have scissors?"

"Yes," I answer, confused.

"Get them for me, if you would." I turn to do so and then stop. I turn to look at him again to determine whether or not he is being serious. "Trust me," he says.

I giggle and rush to retrieve the scissors from the kitchen. I return to the living room and hand the scissors to Eli. He takes the daisy from me and clips the stem. Without saying a word, he gently pushes my hair aside and slides the stem behind my ear so that it is concealed by my brown hair. His touch feels perfect.

Eli takes me to the only French bistro downtown. He holds the door for me, and as we stand in the entranceway waiting to be seated, I feel his hand on the small of my back. Once we're seated, I take a drink of water as Eli orders a bottle of white wine. I melt when he looks at me.

"What?"

"Nothing. You're beautiful, is all."

"I can't believe this."

"What can't you believe?"

"How wonderful this feels."

"Did you expect something else?" He takes a drink from his water after he asks.

"I don't know what I expected. But this feels…right."

"I'm glad, Franki. You're a special person."

The candle between us sends small beads of wax dripping down its side. We don't talk much during dinner. It's not an awkward silence, though. Periodically he looks at me, and I smile. I'm happy with Eli. He treats me like I want to be treated. I want more than anything to trust his intentions. I have no reason not to. I've known him most of my life.

"Remember when we held hands on the bus during the field trip to Columbus in sixth grade?" He pours another glass of wine for both of us.

"Of course I do. I remember it very clearly. You told me not to tell anyone, and when I told Kevin, you didn't talk to me for a year."

"Oh my God, it wasn't a year."

"It felt like it."

"It was more like the summer. I had to teach you a lesson." Eli reaches for me and squeezes my hand. I feel a tingle as he pulls his touch from me. He takes a drink of wine.

***

I hold Eli's hand as we walk downtown after dinner. I feel a little buzzed from the wine. I rest my head on his shoulder. We walk by a bar. There is a band playing.

"Do you want to go inside?" I ask as I look up at him.

"Not really; do you?"

"I don't care."

He pulls me close to him. I wrap my arms around his neck and kiss his cheek. His hands rest on my hips. Then he pulls me into him.

"What are you doing?" I laugh as Eli begins to dance with me right on the sidewalk. "You're crazy!"

His cheek touches mine as he whispers, "I promise I won't tell any-one," into my ear.

"I don't care who knows," I whisper back.

We dance on the sidewalk as patrons enter and exit the bar, staring at us as if we're mad. Maybe we are, but it feels sublime. When the song finishes, we walk to the fountain, and Eli kisses my cheek as we watch the water spill from the top of a huge black rock. The water crashes from the rugged sides of the stone into a pool of water that appears artificially blue.

"Here, take one," Eli commands as he hands me a penny.

"What for?"

"To make a wish, silly. I'll toss one into the water too." He closes his eyes deliberately and flips the coin into the water. The penny produces a small splash, followed by ripples that quickly dissipate.

My knees are weak. "What did you wish for?" I ask.

"I can't tell you. Are you going to make one?"

I close my eyes and drop the penny into the water. I open my eyes and look at the distorted face of the penny as it settles at the bottom of the fountain by one of the yellow lamps illuminating the water. I hope my wish comes true. I want to be loved.

CHAPTER NINE
Late-Night Visit

Ryah Klein

The scenario has unfolded innumerable times before, but this time it feels different. There's something about him. There's something about the way he looks at me, as if he wants me but doesn't need me. That's what makes him sexy. Most men surrender their wills to me to get what they desire. They use me. I know that's what they're doing, but I don't care. I'm using them too, and usually as long as we're both aware that pleasure is the only objective, there remains nothing left once we're finished. Sex doesn't mean anything. It only serves as a temporary distraction until the empty feeling returns. But he's different. He maintains his dignity, and that's what makes me want to please him in every way. I want to submit to him. I want to be his. I want him to think about me when he's alone.

It's late and I am wearing my satin blue lingerie. I need him to want me. It's not good enough for him to say it. I need to see the lust in his eyes. I hear a car park along the road in front of my apartment complex. I look out my window to see him approaching my building. I have butterflies in my stomach. It's really going to happen.

I open the door as soon as he knocks, and I stand in the doorway. The lights in the living room are off, but the hallway light is bright enough that the outline of my body is visible. Eli starts to say something but can't. He's frozen. I don't want him to talk. I reach out to him. He takes my hand, and I lead him inside my apartment. I feel his lips on my neck as I slam the door shut behind him. Eli forces me against the wall, and for the first time, his lips meet mine. We become a frenzy of kissing, licking, and biting until I hear my bra rip and Eli's warm hands are touching my bare skin. My eyes roll back as I concentrate only on the pleasure I feel when he touches me. I want to give him every part of me.

***

I use my fingertip to trace Eli's ribs as he breathes in bed. His scent is all over me and I love it. We still haven't said a word to one another, but it doesn't matter. Our bodies communicated what could never be articulated with words.

"What are you thinking about?" I ask as I reach for his hand and squeeze it.

"I'm not really thinking about anything. How about you?"

"I'm still trying to process everything." I let out a subtle laugh, and Eli turns his head to face me.

"You're amazing," he declares.

"I think you are. I don't know the last time…" I stop myself, not wanting to make it sound like I sleep around.

"I'm sorry I tore your bra."

"Don't be. I was waiting for this all day. I couldn't stop thinking about you. I was sure you wouldn't show."

"Why do you say that?"

"It's how it usually goes for me. I always miss out on everything that is good. There's always something that happens that keeps me from being happy."

"Are you happy now?"

"More than I have been in a long time." I kiss Eli's shoulder and then look at him. His blank expression worries me.

"I'm glad. I couldn't resist you. I'm not sure what it is, but you're not like most women."

"Is that a good thing?" I hate my insecurity.

"I think that it is. It must be, because I had to have you."

I put my arm around Eli and hug him after he says this. He rolls over and kisses my lips gently.

I run my left hand from his chest down his abdomen. "I hope you still want me after tonight."

"I will. Don't worry." He kisses me again, but this time with more force.

"Eli, I think Franki likes you."

"You do?"

"Yes. In fact, that day on the patio, she told me she had a crush on you."

"Why do you bring that up?" He rolls so he's on his back again. I move closer to him and lay my head on his arm.

"I thought you should know since she's my friend. I don't want her to get upset with me."

"Oh. Well, I don't plan to tell her. Do you?"

I feel ashamed after he says this, but I'm not sure why. "Of course not."

"I think it's best for everyone if we keep this between us for a while. I just moved back to town, and the last thing I want is to hear a bunch of rumors about us."

"I agree," I say, even though I want to announce to everyone in town that Eli will be mine. "There are always rumors. It's the curse of a small town."

"Rumors only add to the confusion. Who's to say what's real and what's not anyway?"

CHAPTER TEN

Why Her?

Bo Schnep

She works in the shoe warehouse office and has probably slept with half of the people who work there. The whole town knows about Ryah Klein, but she maintains an allure that goes beyond her good looks. I used to see her jogging in town and wondered what it would feel like to have her in my arms. I never understood why she was rarely in a relationship. I heard that she changed a few summers after she graduated from high school. I don't know why, and I probably never will.

Ryah is wearing a striped pink button-down dress shirt with black pants that accentuate her slender legs. Her black closed-toe heels are shiny and look pricey. I watch her approach the diner and wonder if I'll ever be able to call her mine. She opens the door and removes her oversize sunglasses from her face and puts them on top of her head. Ryah is sexy even when she's not trying.

She spots me sitting at the booth in the far corner of the restaurant and smiles at me. I watch her walk and feel an aching need for her. She sits across from me in the booth and places her small purse on the edge of the table.

"How have you been, Bo?" She sounds distracted while asking.

"I've been doing well. How about you?"

She finally settles herself and looks at me. "Busy as usual, but I can't complain." The waitress comes over and Ryah orders a water with lemon. "Why did you want to see me?"

Suddenly I feel queasy. I don't know if I should reveal to Ryah why I wanted to talk with her. I am afraid she will dismiss it, and maybe me. "I want to tell you—"

"Excuse me. Could I have a straw?" she asks a young busboy. He looks over his shoulder to ensure she is speaking to him and then reflexively searches the pockets of his uniform for a straw. He doesn't have one. Ryah flashes a smile, and the young boy nods his head and rushes to the counter to get one. "I'm sorry, Bo. What were you saying?"

"No problem. I was saying that—"

The busboy returns and hands the straw to Ryah. He's still unable to speak. She delicately pulls it from his grip. I don't think he even realizes that I'm sitting across from her. Ryah says, "You're a darling." The busboy responds with a stupid grin and saunters away while looking over his shoulder. Ryah returns her attention to me as if the whole episode never happened.

I sigh. "Never mind."

"What?" she asks.

"Nothing."

Ryah unwraps her straw and plunges it into her water. She squeezes the lemon until her water turns murky and then drops the lemon into the glass and uses the straw to push the lemon past the ice to the bottom of her glass. I watch this and realize I'm less important to her than her drink.

"Don't be like that, Bo."

"Be like what?"

The waitress returns and apologizes for not bringing Ryah a straw. Ryah orders a salad with crackers. I'm no longer hungry.

As soon as the waitress leaves, Ryah snaps at me, "You ask me to lunch and now you're not hungry?" as if she's embarrassed. I don't respond, and Ryah rolls her eyes. The waitress refills Ryah's water as the busboy smiles at her from behind the counter. It's at that exact moment that I decide I no longer have anything to lose.

"Ryah, we need to talk."

Ryah pulls her cell phone from her purse and starts typing a text. "Go ahead, I'm listening to you."

"Can you put your goddamn phone down and quit acting like I don't matter?"

Ryah looks at me with wide eyes. It is the first time I have ever seen Ryah look stunned. I enjoy her temporary loss of control. It makes me feel empowered.

"What is going on with us?" I demand to know, although Ryah has already regained her composure.

"Bo, what in the hell are you talking about?" She sets her phone on table and looks directly at me. Her eyes appear eager for a challenge. I sometimes believe she thinks life is one big game.

"Don't act that way," I plead.

"What way?"

"This way."

"And what way is that?"

I stare back at her. I don't detect any emotion from her whatsoever. My stomach sinks.

"What are we doing?" I restate my question. I hope she will calm down and talk to me.

"We aren't doing anything, Bo. Why would you think that we are?"

"We are…" I stop talking when I realize my voice is raised. I shake my head and take a deep breath. I begin in a softer voice. "We are fucking each other, Ryah. That's something."

She smiles. "I guess that it is. Why are you always so serious?" The waitress brings the salad and places it on the table. As soon as the waitress leaves our table, Ryah unfolds her napkin and places it on her lap. She then proceeds to mix the ingredients on her plate with her fork.

Ryah dips her fork into a small bowl of fat-free vinaigrette dressing and takes a small bite of lettuce. She chews it and then looks up at me. No matter how angry I am, I can't deny that I care for her.

"Please tell me that there's something more going on here than just that."

"Bo, we talked about this. I told you from the beginning that I'm not looking for a relationship. Remember? I told you I would be honest with you, and you said you understood." She takes another bite of lettuce and then takes a drink of water.

"I know. I remember. But don't you feel anything?" Ryah looks at me. "I mean, do you think you would ever want something more?"

"I can't say. I don't know what I want right now," she replies.

"OK."

Ryah sets her fork on the edge of her plate. "Are you mad at me?" Her blue eyes look so pure.

"No."

"Are you sure?"

"No."

"Ha-ha. Oh, Bo. Relax! Enjoy life a bit. Is your job stressing you out?"

"Not at all." I take a drink from my coffee. It's lukewarm.

"Should we stop seeing each other?"

"That's not what I'm saying, Ryah."

"What are you saying, then?"

"I care for you." Ryah doesn't say anything. She pushes her plate away from her. "Is that so bad? Is it so bad to care about you?"

She doesn't respond. Her flat expression upsets me.

"Damn it!"

The waitress returns, and Ryah asks for a box. She uses her fork to push the rest of her salad into the Styrofoam container and closes the lid. Ryah drinks the rest of her water. When the waitress delivers the bill, I hand her my credit card. Ryah doesn't even offer to pay.

"We've shared some great times, Ryah. Remember that. You like me for moments."

Ryah checks her phone. "Moments are all anyone can hope for. We have to do our best to enjoy them."

CHAPTER ELEVEN
Who Cares?

Kasey Price

Everything looks the same, but it isn't. I sit in my car and look at her apartment building while thinking about all the times I took her for granted. I can see the light in her bedroom is on. The blinds are drawn, but I know she's awake. She's not expecting me. The last time I saw her, she said she never wanted to see me again. I don't think she meant it, though. People rarely mean what they say.

I walk to the front door and take a deep breath before I knock. I don't hear anything, so I knock again. Just as I'm about to lose my courage, I hear movement inside. The door opens, and Franki stands there, unable to speak. She's wearing a white tank top and jeans that sit low on her hips. Her hair is not styled, but it looks sexy.

"I'm sorry to drop by unannounced, but I had to see you," I reveal. Franki doesn't say anything. "May I come in?"

"I...sure." She hesitates for a moment before she moves aside and invites me in. I walk past her and stand in the entranceway. The familiarity is eerie. I stayed in this very same apartment so many times, and now I feel like a stranger.

"Can I get you something to drink?"

"Yes. I'll have a glass of water, if you don't mind."

"Not a problem." Franki walks to the kitchen. I notice her bare feet and remember when she used to sit next to me on the couch and paint her toenails while I watched television. It seemed so meaningless then.

Franki hands me a glass of water and invites me to have a seat in the living room. I can tell she is confused, but I know she doesn't want to ask why I'm here. Franki is too nice sometimes.

"How have you been, Franki?" I take another drink and look at her. She begins to twirl her hair nervously.

"I've been well. I haven't seen you in a while. How have you been?"

"I know. It's been too long. I guess I can't complain." I take another drink and set the glass on her end table, making sure it rests on a coaster. "I don't know why I visited tonight."

"I've thought about visiting you too at times."

"Why haven't you?"

"Because it would be too hard."

"Why? We used to be so close."

"That was then."

"I guess you're right. It's difficult to process how one day you're with a person and the next day you're not. I never could grasp that concept."

"I know." She looks away at nothing in particular. She's still twirling her hair. I can see her ribs through her white shirt as she breathes.

"What happened to us?"

Franki turns her head and looks at me. "I don't know."

"Why did we ever stop talking? I mean, we were good together."

"We were. But then there was the…" She stops and turns away.

"The what?"

She takes a deep breath. "Don't make me say it."

"Say what? I don't know what you're going to say."

"The issue."

"What issue?"

"The trust issue."

"There was never a trust issue." I lean forward. She is looking at me again. Her eyes look sad.

"Not for you. There wasn't a trust issue for you. You never had to worry about trusting me. It was you I worried about. You would never give me a straight answer. Remember? There's no way you could have forgotten."

"I didn't forget, Franki. It's just that I thought it would all be over once you realized there was nothing to worry about."

"How would I know if there was or was not something to worry about when you would never talk to me truthfully? All you would give me was vague answers until I couldn't take the uncertainty any longer. I don't deserve to be unhappy. God, why are you doing this to me?" Her breathing is irregular and I see tears in the corners of her eyes. She closes her eyes and massages her eyelids with her fingertips.

"Don't get upset. That's not why I came here."

She opens her eyes and in a louder voice asks, "Why *did* you come here?"

"I needed to see you. I miss you."

"Stop."

"I mean it."

"Kasey. Don't…" She puts her head down. Her breathing is shallow. I stand up and walk over to her.

"I'm serious."

"Don't do this."

"Come here." I grab her right wrist lightly before she pulls away. "Franki…" I grab her wrist again, and this time she goes limp. I guide her to stand up, which she does reluctantly. I hug her and can feel her tears wetting my black T-shirt. I say, "Don't cry," which only makes her cry more. She's sobbing and I'm hugging her with more force. She finally wraps her arms around my neck and hugs me back. We hold each other for a minute or so, and then I back away from her slowly and look down at her. Franki's eyes are red. I lean down, and before she can reject my advance, I kiss her lips. She pulls away. I lean down again.

"Kasey, we can't do this."

"Franki, I care for you."

"I care for you too, but we can't do this."

"Why not?"

"It's over."

I lean down again, but Franki turns her head away from me.

"I think you should leave."

"Franki—" I begin.

"Kasey, please. Please, just leave."

"I'm sorry."

"So am I," she says in a trembling voice. I look at her and then turn and leave her apartment. She closes the door behind me without any good-bye. In my car, I text Ryah, "Can I come over?"

CHAPTER TWELVE
Who is This?

Scarlett Davison

It feels strange, but it shouldn't. He's still next to me in bed. I can hear him breathing. We stare at the ceiling. Neither of us says anything. I guess there's nothing to say. I wanted it to happen. I shouldn't feel guilty. I've been single for almost two years. He is the first guy I have been with since I moved back to Payne. I think he really likes me. That should mean something. I'm not sure that it does. I'm not sure of anything any longer. *Why do I feel guilty?*

I get out of bed and put on Bo's white dress shirt. I button two buttons and then walk to the kitchen without saying anything to Bo. I can feel his eyes watching me as I leave the room. He makes me feel sexy. I pour myself a glass of cold water and take a drink. I set the glass on the counter and place butter in the skillet as I prepare the cheese and bread. I finish making two sandwiches and put them into the skillet. They sizzle as I make sure to flip them before placing them onto a plate and cutting them diagonally. I pour a glass of water for Bo and grab his plate. I used to make this exact meal all the time for my ex. It's funny how we do the same things for different people.

Bo smiles when he sees me enter the bedroom with a grilled cheese sandwich on one of my grandmother's antique porcelain plates. I hand him the plate and warn him the sandwich is still hot. He takes the plate from me, and then I hand him the glass of water. He takes a drink.

"You're so wonderful."

"Thank you."

"I mean it. I love grilled cheese sandwiches."

"I'm glad."

"You even cut them diagonally."

"Isn't that the only way to cut a grilled cheese sandwich?" I ask playfully.

"It should be. This is the perfect Saturday."

I sit on the bed next to Bo and watch him. He smiles at me and takes a bite of his sandwich. A string of cheese hangs from the bread and sticks to Bo's chin. Even with his blond hair tousled and cheese stuck to his face, he's still handsome. I want to like him more than I do. I hope that I can.

I wash the dishes as Bo sits in the living room with some television program blaring in the background. I finish the dishes and walk into the living room to find Bo texting on his phone. I sit by him. He doesn't look up.

"Can we turn the television off?"

"Why?"

"Because you're not watching it."

"I was watching it. What would you rather do?"

I reach for the remote and turn the television off. "That's better. How can you stand to have the volume turned up like that?"

"It doesn't bother me."

I turn on my stereo and put on an old vinyl. The songs are slow and sad.

"Why do you listen to such sad music?"

"I guess it calms me. Don't you like it?"

Bo's phone vibrates, and he picks it up from his lap and checks the message. "Not really. It's depressing."

"Sometimes life is depressing."

"That may be true, but I don't want to dwell on sadness. Why do you?"

"I don't know. I suppose it makes me appreciate the good times a little more. You can't have any good without some bad, you know."

Bo types a message and sets his phone down on the arm of the couch. "I guess you're right."

I watch Bo finish his text conversation with someone that he never bothers to identify. He then starts playing some game on his phone. I lie on the carpet in the living room and close my eyes. The music washes over me, and even though Bo sits just feet away from me, I feel alone. I think about the time before I moved to Payne when I was madly in love and moments like this one didn't feel so empty. I never used to own a television. I didn't need one. All I would do was listen to record after record with the man that I loved. We imagined ourselves in the songs. They became part of our life together. Often we would be doing something and one of us would recite a verse from one of those old records that fit the mood perfectly. I wish it would have ended differently. I miss him.

As I reminisce about the time he gave me a flower and told me to wear it behind my ear on our date, the music stops playing. I open my eyes and sit up.

"Why did you turn the music off?"

"Oh…I thought you were taking a nap. I'm sorry."

"I'm not napping."

"I'm sorry."

"Don't worry about it."

"Are you sure?"

"Yes."

Bo reaches for the remote and turns the television on again. He turns the volume down, but it still annoys me. I get up and walk to the bedroom to grab my phone. I check for new text messages to find that I don't have any. I sit on the edge of the bed. I want to text him. I know I shouldn't want to, but I do. It's wrong. Bo is in the other room. I wonder if he still thinks of me. I shouldn't text him.

I send a text message that simply says, "How are you?" I feel so anxious after I send the message that I can't catch my breath. I try to calm myself while standing in the doorway of the bedroom. I remove Bo's shirt and put on a pair of shorts and a tank top. I carry my phone into the living room and find Bo talking to one of his detective friends about some ongoing bet they have about Mrs. Claybrook's aggressive dogs and how many people they will bite this year. He is reclined on the couch, still shirtless, and is laughing about whatever his friend just said. I stop and stand in front of him. He looks at me and smiles. My phone vibrates in my hand. I don't check it. I'm too nervous to see if it's him. Maybe it's better not to know. It was a mistake. I shouldn't have texted him. I walk closer to Bo. I lean down and kiss him once on the lips. He pulls my head closer with his left hand and kisses me again. I want to check my phone, but I don't. I sit next to Bo and wait for him to finish his conversation. My phone vibrates again. I look down at my clenched hand. I push the home button to reveal the message. It says, "Who is this?"

CHAPTER THIRTEEN
It Happens so Fast

Franki Rose

"I like this," Eli says as we lie on the floor in his living room listening to music.

"I do too. It's so calming. I don't know why I have never done this."

"Close your eyes."

"Why?"

"Do it. Close your eyes. The music is so much better." I close my eyes. Eli is right. I can hear every nuance with perfect clarity. I feel weightless. I can hear Eli shifting to my left. I open my eyes when I feel his lips press against mine. Eli looks down at me. I smile and then pull him to me and kiss him.

"What are you thinking?" Eli asks. I can feel his body pressed against mine.

"I'm thinking about how right this feels."

"I have a terrible past with women."

I look at Eli. He is no longer looking at me. Instead he is staring at something that isn't there. "What do you mean by that?"

"I'm not trying to upset you, but I want you to know. I've been hurt in the past and I've done my share of hurting."

"I think we all have, Eli. Haven't we?"

"I suppose you're right. I don't want to mislead you. I want to avoid hurting you."

"You won't hurt me, Eli. I know you, remember?"

"Do you? I mean, you know parts of me. You know who I was in high school. But do you really know me?"

"Why are you saying this?"

"Because I want you to know the risk of getting involved with me."

"We don't need to know everything about someone to know them, Eli. Don't be so cynical." I turn my head and look at Eli. His face is emotionless. "Here, come with me."

"What are you doing?"

I stand up and reach my hands down to him. "Trust me."

"That's something that doesn't come easily for me."

"Please. I won't hurt you."

"That's not what scares me."

I lean down and grab his hands. I feel his grip tighten, and I start to lean back until he stands the rest of the way up. "Come on."

I lead Eli down the hallway to his bedroom. I kiss his lips but pull back when he tries to kiss me back. "No. Let me lead." I kiss him again. This time he doesn't kiss me back. I feel his grip tightening around my right hand. I lean in and kiss him, this time with more force. He lets go of my hand, and I pull back.

"Eli, I'm going to show you can trust me." He doesn't say anything. I kiss his lips once more. This time I gently suck his lower lip. I grip his arm with my hand. I can feel his muscles tensing. I push him gently backward so that he sits on the bed. I look down at him and smile.

"Are you sure you want to do this?" he asks in a barely audible voice.

I straddle his legs and put my hands on his shoulders. I can feel him squirming. The next time I lean down to kiss him, he pulls me on top of him. It all happens so fast.

***

I'm left paralyzed by my pleasure. Eli is still on top of me with his head resting on my chest. I can feel his body shaking. I run my hand through his hair. His back is glistening with sweat. The moonlight shining through his bedroom makes his shadowed body look perfect. Eli rolls off of me. I can hear him breathing. He doesn't say anything. I don't either. I don't want to ruin the moment.

"Does this change anything?" I finally ask after our breathing has returned to normal. I lick my lips and savor the salty taste.

"Why would it?"

"I don't know. It's just..." I stop talking for some reason. I feel like I might cry. I start blinking to keep the tears from escaping.

"What?" he asks.

I take a deep breath. Luckily it's too dark for Eli to see my face; otherwise, I would be mortified. "Never mind."

"You can tell me, Franki."

"I don't know if I should."

"Please."

"I don't think I should." I turn over in bed so that I'm facing away from Eli. I want him to put an arm around me and promise me everything will be OK. I want to know he cares about me. I need to hear him say it.

"Why are you being like this?"

"I'm sorry," I say, feeling my lip tremble a bit.

"There's nothing to be sorry about, Franki. I want to know what you started to say."

"I'm scared, Eli."

"Why? There's nothing to be scared of." I need him to touch me. I have to feel him.

"I like you. There. I said it. I like you. That's what scares me." I wait for Eli to respond. I feel the bed shift. I turn over in bed in time to see Eli walk out of the room.

CHAPTER FOURTEEN
Do I Know You?

Elijah Noor

I wonder how other people see me. I want to know more than what they would tell me if I asked them that question. I want to know their impressions and deepest thoughts beyond the boring sentiments restrained by civility. I don't think anyone would see the same person. Maybe there are only pieces of me.

I find myself at the Conversation Bar on Oak Street drinking a draft beer and wanting to disappear. It's a little after midnight on a Thursday evening. I couldn't stay at Wayside any longer. I had to get away. That's the irony, though. I can never disappear in this town. No matter where I go, people know me. I hear the front door open and see a slender woman in her early twenties enter. She looks around before taking a seat at the far end of the bar. I watch her as she orders a mixed drink. When the bartender delivers the drink, she stirs it with her straw slowly. Her long dark hair and her tan skin make her look exotic. She doesn't appear as though she belongs here. I continue to watch her. Eventually she notices that I'm looking at her. She smiles. My expression doesn't change. I'm fascinated by her because I don't recognize her, and that makes her even more attractive to me.

After she finishes her second drink, she gets up from her stool and walks over to the jukebox. I watch her as she scrolls through the song selections. She looks over her shoulder at me and then looks back at the jukebox screen. I order another beer. She knows I'm watching her. She selects another song and waits until it starts playing before she walks back to her seat. I no longer care about what I should or should not do. All that matters to me is what actually happens. Intention stopped mattering years ago.

Her forearm touches mine as she leans in and thanks me for ordering her another drink. Derek, the bartender, and I have known each other since grade school, when we had the same music class together and I talked him into calling the teacher a bitch. We laugh about it now. Everything loses its meaning over time.

"What's your name?" I ask. I observe that her eyes are already glassy and she's smiling with more frequency.

"Katy Beckford. What's your name?"

"Eli Noor. It's a pleasure to meet you."

"Likewise." She takes a drink and looks straight ahead in an attempt to not appear too eager. I smile when I recognize her effort.

"So are you from here?" she eventually asks after I stop paying attention to her.

"Yes, I am. How about yourself?" I take a drink from my beer and appear distracted, which causes her to become more interested.

She tosses her hair over her shoulder and fiddles with her cell phone. "I'm not from here. I'm visiting my sister. I'm from Chicago."

"That's cool," I say in the most emotionless tone I can muster. "I hope you are enjoying yourself." She doesn't immediately respond. I take the opportunity to joke with Derek about a girl he was trying to pick up a few weeks ago. He laughs and shrugs his shoulders. Katy becomes agitated by my inattention. She sends a few text messages and then takes a long drink and offers and audible sigh.

"Is there anything to do in this town?" she asks.

"I don't know. I guess it depends on what you're looking for."

"Anything would be better than this."

"Where are you staying tonight?"

Katy's face relaxes. She hesitates as she tries to decipher the meaning behind my question. I don't offer any clarification.

"With my sister," she relays defiantly.

"Well, I ask because that determines where I can direct you." Katy offers a nervous smile in response. Her confusion is apparent. She can't read me at all.

***

I play music on my phone as we walk to my apartment. There is a full moon overhead, and the summer air is thick with humidity.

"I love this song!" she exclaims drunkenly as she starts to twirl slowly in a circle. I stop and grab her when she nearly falls over. We both laugh. "I'm sorry. I guess I'm a little tipsy."

"It's OK. You're on vacation. You're supposed to have fun."

Katy throws her arms around me and hugs me tightly. "I like you," she proclaims in my ear. I pull my head away from her and she giggles.

"Thank you. Let's get you to my place safely."

"Do you have anything to drink at your place?"

"I have some white wine."

"Yay! Wait, let's listen to that one song again."

Once we're at my apartment, I pour Katy a glass of wine and play some music. She takes a drink, leans back in the chair, and closes her eyes while smiling to herself.

"This is such a sad song. Do you have anything more upbeat?" she asks.

"Not really."

"What do you do? I mean, what kind of work do you do? You do have a job, don't you?"

"I do have a job," I say.

"What kind of job? I work in finance. It's horrible."

"I'm sorry to hear that. I manage my father's restaurant. It's equally horrible." Katy leans forward to take a drink but instead accidently spills wine on the front of her green blouse.

"Oops. I'm so clumsy."

"Don't worry about it. I'll get you a towel." I walk to the closet and grab a washcloth. I wet it in the bathroom sink.

"I think your job sounds fun," she yells from the living room. "I wish I could do a job like that. My parents insisted I go to college. I shouldn't complain. I've always envied those who do what they want."

I reenter the living room and hand her the towel. She fumbles with it and rubs at her blouse and then tosses the towel on the floor.

"Come here and kiss me," she demands in a playful voice. I walk over to her and hold out my hand. "What?" she asks.

"Give me your hand." She does so reluctantly and I guide her out of the chair. She looks up at me. I look into her eyes. Her simple expression and deep breaths indicate she knows what is about to happen. I kiss her lips gently. I pull back and look at her. Her eyes are closed and her face looks frozen from the embrace.

"I want to stay here tonight," she says as she opens her eyes.

"Do you think that's a good idea?"

"I don't care if it is or isn't. I want to be close to you. There's something about you."

"What do you mean?"

"You're not like most guys I meet. There's a sweetness to you. Don't worry, it's a compliment."

"I'm not who you think I am."

"Who are you?"

CHAPTER FIFTEEN
Those Who are Closest

Ryah Klein

I can't stop thinking about him. I find myself lying in bed for hours watching my ceiling fan rotate while thinking of how his skin feels against mine. I haven't washed my sheets since his last visit. I spent the next few nights enjoying his lingering scent on my pillow. I have to see him. I can't take it any longer. *Why doesn't he call me?* I'm sure there is a reason. I always want the one who is unavailable.

I decide to go see him at Wayside. I'm not sure I can disguise my intent. I want him in every way. I fix my hair while looking at myself in the mirror and unbutton another button on my violet blouse to reveal my white tank top underneath. I decide against wearing a belt so that my worn jeans will hang low off my hips. I tousle my hair one last time so that I don't look overly concerned about my appearance. My body aches for him.

I approach him with purpose. His eyes fix on mine as I sit directly in front of him at the bar. He is wearing a blue button-down shirt that is unbuttoned enough to reveal his chest, which is tan and without any blemish. His black hair isn't styled. Eli's lack of concern for how others view him is what makes him so attractive.

"How are you, Ryah? I haven't heard from you."

"I thought I would surprise you."

"I'm glad you did."

His eyes are still staring into mine. I can't help but smirk when I consider our undeniable connection to one another. "Where have you been? I've missed you."

"I'm sorry. My father hasn't been doing very well. I've had to take on more hours here."

"I didn't know. You should have told me."

"It wouldn't have changed anything, Ryah. It's something I have to deal with."

"I know, but I could be there for you. I want to be there for you if you need me."

"That's very kind of you to say that." He diverts his attention from me as a couple enters the bar. "Excuse me for a second." He walks over to the couple, who sit at a table positioned along the wall. I watch him in the mirror on the back wall of the bar. The casual confidence he displays makes my skin tingle. I want him so badly.

"I apologize for that," he relays as he fixes two drinks for the couple. I act as though his departure didn't matter. Whenever I become aware of how easily other people can influence my self-esteem, I feel an agonizing anxiety that makes me feel uncomfortable with myself. I hate feeling vulnerable.

Eli returns from delivering the drinks to the couple and leans on the bar in front of me. "Drinking tonight?"

"I'll have a bottle of beer."

"I didn't take you for the type of girl who drinks beer."

I smile. "I've been known to surprise people every now and then."

He laughs. "I imagine that is very true. You are something else, Ryah." He twists the cap off a bottle of beer and places it in front of me.

"Thank you," I say before I take a drink. Eli walks away and takes a few additional orders from patrons playing a card game. He appears distracted. *Why won't he give me his full attention?*

"Would you like another drink?" Eli asks as he takes my empty bottle and tosses it in the trash. I hear the glass shatter, and it causes me to wince.

"I don't think so. I didn't really come here to drink." Eli stops wiping the bar with the towel in his hands and looks at me.

"Oh yeah? Why did you come here then?" Eli asks as he smiles at me.

"To see what time you will be done with work tonight."

His smile fades as his expression becomes more serious. "Why do you want to know?"

"You're going to make me say it, aren't you?"

"Say what?" He begins fidgeting with the towel.

"Eli, Eli, Eli. I refuse to believe you are this innocent, but it's an endearing gesture."

He tosses the towel over his shoulder. "Ryah, I'm not sure—"

I interrupt him. "I want you to visit tonight after work."

"Oh. I don't know if I can."

I feel my stomach turn. "Oh, OK."

"It's not what you think. It's my father."

"I understand."

"Listen, don't react that way. I want to visit you again." His hand touches mine as it rests on the bar. I savor his touch for a moment and then pull my hand away. "I will visit you soon," he promises.

I want to run out of the bar, but instead I get up and walk slowly out without saying anything else to Eli. I can sense him watching me walk away and that satisfies me. I wait until I am outside again before I call Kasey.

"Hello," he says when he answers after the second ring.

"I don't know what to do," I say.

"What's wrong, Ryah?"

"Everything. I don't know."

"Where are you?"

"I'm leaving Wayside."

"Are you going home?"

Eli's rejection stings more with every question Kasey asks me. "I don't know. I guess."

"I'll be right over. Everything will be OK, Ryah."

CHAPTER SIXTEEN

Somewhere Else

Bo Schnep

Scarlett looks beautiful sitting across from me at Danny's Bistro on Townline and Main. Her shoulder-length black hair is straight and looks magnificent in the dim light. She takes a drink from her coffee and smiles at me. The red dress she is wearing makes her fair skin appear absolutely flawless. I want to be with a person who cares about me as much as I care about them.

"How has your week gone?" she asks before taking another sip from her coffee. Our server arrives and places our salads in front of us. I'm not hungry at all.

"It's been pretty calm so far. Most weeks here are, though."

She giggles. "I suppose you're right. That's just one of the many joys of small towns. Everything is calm on the surface."

I look at Scarlett to find her staring at me. I'm not sure why. "I think you're right."

Scarlett places her napkin on her lap and starts using her fork to pick through her salad. I place my napkin on my lap too, but I don't even bother with the salad. I take a drink of water and hear a slow song playing in the background that causes me to realize that life is merely a series of moments that will eventually be over.

"I've been happy lately," Scarlett blurts before she starts eating.

"I'm glad to hear that. I was worried about you."

"I've dealt with a lot in the last few years, but I think I'm finally recovering. You have been great to me." She appears embarrassed to admit something so personal.

"Scarlett, you are incredible."

Scarlett smiles. "Thank you. You are so sweet."

"Will you ever feel comfortable telling me what happened that caused you to be so sad?"

"I think I will when I resolve it with myself. My sadness was caused by loss and my inability to accept it." I nod and look at my salad. I push it aside and take another drink of water. "Does it bother you that I haven't felt comfortable sharing some of my past?"

"I think everyone is haunted by their past in some way. The key is that we don't allow the past to deter us from enjoying the present."

"I agree wholeheartedly. I'm so happy to be here with you."

"I'm happy too." I pull my phone from my pocket and check it before returning it to my pocket.

"It's not work, is it?" It is evident to me that her concern isn't about me but the possibility of finishing dinner alone.

"No, it's not work. I thought I felt it vibrate, but it didn't."

Our server delivers our entrées and I inspect mine. The fettuccini Alfredo looks appetizing but I don't feel like eating. Scarlett cuts her ravioli and then looks up at me.

"Is something wrong?" She looks genuinely worried.

"Not at all. I just remembered this detail for court on Tuesday. Do you mind?" I ask as I pull my phone from my pocket again. I can see her worry transition into frustration.

"Go ahead." She starts eating her ravioli.

I text Ryah, "Can I see you?" I don't know why I feel compelled to see her. I want to wait on her to respond, but instead I place my phone back inside my pocket.

"Feel better?" Scarlett asks.

"Yes. Thank you."

Scarlett and I don't say much on the ride back to her house. I get out and walk her to the door.

"Would you like to come in?" she asks.

I feel for my phone in my pocket. It hasn't vibrated. "I don't know if I should."

Scarlett reaches for my hand and then opens her door and leads me inside. "It's OK," she says before she kisses me on the lips. "I want to be with you."

I kiss her. "I want to be with you too." I feel my phone vibrate in my pocket.

"Come with me." Scarlett takes my hand and directs me to her bedroom. She stops beside her bed and turns to face me. I remove my blazer and put it on a chair in the corner of her bedroom. My eyes haven't acclimated to the darkness. When I turn to face her, I feel her lips against mine. I pull her toward me. She kisses me with more passion. I caress her hair and then push a strand behind her ear. Scarlett leans into my touch so that her head tilts to the side. I kiss her neck. She smells so good. I rub my cheek against her skin. I grab her waist and turn her around so that I can unzip her dress. It falls from her body to the floor. Scarlett's simple beauty and shy demeanor remind me of a nude model preparing to be painted.

"I want you," I whisper in her ear. I am holding her arms and can feel her shaking.

"I want you too." I unbutton my shirt. Her fingertips massage my chest as I throw my shirt to the floor. "Come here," she commands as she eases onto the bed. I approach her slowly. Her anticipation is apparent.

***

Scarlett goes to the bathroom after we finish. I can hear the water running. I get out of bed and reach for my blazer on the chair. I take my phone from the pocket. I have one text message from Ryah that says, "Visit me tomorrow and don't tell anyone." My breath leaves me. Scarlett returns.

"Are you OK?" she asks.

"I've never been better."

CHAPTER SEVENTEEN

In a Daze

Franki Rose

Birds sing even when the world is filled with sadness. I don't know why people can't do the same thing. The park is empty except for two teenage boys hanging near the edge of the woods. They keep looking at me as if they are checking to see if I am watching them. One of them pulls a pack of cigarettes from his pants pocket. I watch as they light the cigarettes and take a few puffs before walking away. I sit on the bench near the swings and watch the squirrels chase one another. *Everyone needs someone, don't they?*

I see Ryah approaching and smile to myself. She is wearing large black sunglasses, a dark-blue blouse, and a short black skirt. Ryah has the body to pull off the outfits I could only dream of wearing. Her small purse hangs loosely from her shoulder. She waves at me when she sees me seated on the bench. I wave back. Ryah is a good friend.

"What are you doing sitting all by your lonesome?" Ryah sits next to me and gives me a hug. I hug her back and feel a weight lift from me.

"I'm waiting on you. You're late."

Ryah stops hugging me. "Only ten minutes. Work has been dreadful lately."

"I'm only kidding you. You look disgustingly pretty."

"I feel like a bloated cow, but thank you. You look good yourself, hot stuff!"

I look down at my pink T-shirt and my plain black shorts. "My legs are fat."

"That's crazy talk, Franki. You look hot." I don't believe Ryah, but her compliment makes me feel better anyway. "So what's up?"

"I don't know. I've been down lately."

"Why? What's wrong?"

"Nothing. Everything. I don't know. Men."

"Aren't men the cause of all of the world's unhappiness?"

"I think you may be right. It's just that…well, I've been seeing Eli recently."

"Really? That's amazing. How's it going?" Ryah repositions herself on the bench. Her knee brushes against mine.

"It's been going well. I mean, he is very sweet to me."

"So what's the problem?"

"I don't know if it's real."

"What do you mean?"

I pause. My throat feels dry. "He seems distracted at times, as if he's there but isn't really. Does that make sense?"

Ryah looks away from me and then faces me again. "Yes, it does."

"I don't know what to do. I like him, but I don't want to make the same mistake I did with Kasey."

"I don't blame you for wanting to be careful. Kasey hurt you pretty badly, and he's an asshole for doing so."

"I've forgiven Kasey. I had to in order to get over him. Ever since him, I've been afraid to trust people. I don't want to be suspicious, but I can't help it."

"I think it's healthy for you to be suspicious of others, especially after being with Kasey. You're smart, Franki. You won't let someone like Kasey hurt you again. You shouldn't feel guilty about wanting to protect yourself."

"It's just not like me to feel this way. I want Eli to want me, but I'm afraid I'm sending the wrong signals."

"I think you should take it slow with Eli. I know you like him, but do you know him?"

"We grew up together."

"But you hadn't seen him in years until recently. People change, Franki. Just be careful. I don't want you getting hurt."

"I appreciate it. I think I will snap out of this soon. It helps to talk about it, though."

"That's what friends are for. I hope you know that I'm always here for you."

"I do, Ryah. You're a true friend."

The two teenagers return and sit at a picnic table. Ryah looks at them. "Do you think we should tell them?" she asks. The teenagers notice Ryah looking at them. I imagine them lusting for her.

"Tell them what?"

"That this life is impossible to understand."

I laugh. "No. I think everyone has to figure that out for themselves."

"I think you may be right, Franki."

I turn toward Ryah. "Can I ask you something?"

"Sure," she assures me.

"I don't want you to get angry."

Ryah places her hand on my bare knee. "Are you kidding? We're friends. You can ask me anything. What is it?"

"Never mind. It's silly. I shouldn't have brought it up."

Ryah frowns. "Don't be like that, Franki. If we're friends, we should be able to talk to one another without feeling awkward or ashamed. What is it?"

"It's not a big deal."

"It must be important or you wouldn't have brought it up."

I clear my throat. "Did you ever see Kasey?"

Ryah's expression doesn't change. Her eyes remain hidden behind her sunglasses. "What do you mean?"

"Did you ever see Kasey? Like, behind my back?"

CHAPTER EIGHTEEN
Tears Sometimes Happen

Elijah Noor

She wants me more than I want her. I can tell by the way she pulls me into her body while I'm lying next to her in bed. Her fingertip tenderly traces the tattoos that cover my upper arm. I can feel her warm breath against my bare back. I want to like her. She's incredibly attractive and an unbelievable lover, but that's all. I lack any real feelings for her, and I don't know why. I want something she doesn't have. Sometimes I think I'll never be happy.

Ryah leans up in bed and rests her chin on my right shoulder. I can feel her breasts touching my back. I don't look at her.

"We're going to have to tell her at some point." Her fingernails gently run the length of my arm. Ryah knows how to please a man. The seductive way she touches me almost makes me forget that I have no genuine feelings for her.

"Tell who what?" I move so that I am now flat on my back. Ryah kisses my chest and then kisses my neck. Her arm is now draped over me.

"We have to tell Franki about us eventually," she says in a hushed voice.

"I don't think that's a good idea." I look at Ryah. Her eyes are busy studying my body.

"I'm not saying we need to tell her now." She bites her lip and then smirks. "But it's something that has to be revealed at some point, don't you think?"

I take a deep breath. "I don't know."

Ryah pulls her hand from me and sits up in bed so that our bodies are no longer touching. "What do you mean by that?" she asks as if she's annoyed by my reluctance.

"I'm saying it won't help anything to admit to Franki that we've been sleeping together. What good would that do?" I turn my head to see Ryah's reaction. All I can detect is annoyance.

She sighs. "I see how it is." She gets out of bed and searches the floor for her panties and bra. Ryah turns away from me as she dresses.

"What are you talking about?"

"Never mind."

"You're impossible," I say before sitting up in bed and reaching for my underwear.

"I'm impossible? Really? You're going to say that while you're in my bed?"

"I said it, didn't I?"

"How can you say that and mean it? You're the one who is treating me badly, not the other way around."

I stand up and start scanning the room for the rest of my clothes. I want to leave. "I don't treat you badly, Ryah. I treat you like you want to be treated."

"You asshole. I can't believe you."

"What the hell can't you believe, Ryah? I come over here to see you, and the only time we get along is when we sleep together. As soon as that's over, you start in with whatever scheme you're working at the time."

"Get out of here. You're not going to insult me in my home." She points toward the door of her bedroom. I walk out of the room. As I button my jeans and slide my blue T-shirt over my head, I hear her plead, "Don't leave."

I stop and turn around to see Ryah rushing out of her bedroom in a panic.

"What do you want? You tell me to leave and then you tell me to stay. What do you want from me?" I ask.

Ryah is breathing heavily. Tears form in her eyes. "I want you." She starts to sob uncontrollably. "Can't you understand that?"

"Calm down, Ryah." I walk toward her.

"Don't touch me unless you mean it. Damn it, Eli. You have to believe in something. You have to feel something."

I put my arms around her and hug her. Her crying becomes even more exaggerated. "What did I do?" I ask. I'm not sure that I care to hear her response.

"I know why you don't want to tell Franki. How stupid do you think I am? Do you think you are smarter than everyone? You may be able to deceive everyone else in this town, but you can't fool me."

I let go of Ryah and take a step backward. "What in the hell are you talking about?"

"Goddamn. Don't insult me. You're seeing Franki. She told me. I heard it from her mouth in the park. I know all about it. I know about you two going on elegant dates and holding hands. I've heard every fucking detail. How do you think that makes me feel, or do you even care?"

"Ryah, I don't see why you're so upset. We're not exclusive. We've never even discussed being exclusive. So what if I've gone on a few dates with Franki? What does that prove?"

"It proves you're just like every other man. You're a lying asshole who feels nothing and wants nothing, except sex."

"That's not fair."

Ryah backs away from me. "It's the truth. Think about it. What I'm saying is true. You take Franki on dates and talk to her like she's a person and then you visit me and all you want to do is fuck. As soon as you're finished, you leave and don't think about me again. I know how men are. You can't tell me any differently. All men are the same."

I shake my head. "If you say so."

"Oh, how shocking. Elijah Noor is shutting down. Wait, wouldn't you have to display a recognizable emotion before we could actually call it shutting down? I should say your uncaring nature is revealing itself gradually. It's difficult to fake life, isn't it?"

"I wouldn't know." I turn from Ryah to walk away. She grabs my arm.

"So that's it? That's all I ever was to you? Someone to fill the time between dates with women you can be seen with in public?"

I look down at her hand gripping my arm. Her knuckles are white. "Let go, Ryah," I say calmly.

"Answer me, damn it. Am I just an object to you?" Her grip tightens and her nails dig into my skin. My arm starts to sting.

"I never know when to take you seriously, Ryah. I thought all you wanted was a little fun. I didn't know you wanted anything else. You're impossible to read." Her grip on my arm loosens.

"Look who's talking." She lets go of my arm. I want to leave her and never see her again, but instead I stand motionlessly and wait for her to do or say something. This moment means very little to me, but I am aware of the potential disaster that could ensue if I handle Ryah improperly.

"What can I do, Ryah?" I ask in a low voice.

"I don't want to feel used," she whimpers.

"I don't want you to feel that way either," I tell her.

"Do you hate me?"

"No. Why would I?" Ryah throws her arms around me and hugs me tightly. Her breathing is exaggerated. I can feel her stomach pressing against mine every time she exhales.

"I don't know. I'm not used to feeling this way," she confesses to me while still hugging me.

"What way are you feeling?"

Ryah's arms relax as she eases from me. "I'm not used to feeling this vulnerable. That's how people feel when they care, Eli. They feel exposed and that causes fear. I'm afraid of you."

I look at Ryah. Her cheeks are wet with tears and her eyes are bloodshot. "You shouldn't be afraid of me," I assert.

"Why shouldn't I be?"

CHAPTER NINETEEN
Where Did He Go?

Ryah Klein

Only fools cry when life hurts. It serves no purpose. All it does is cause the people who witness the tears to feel pity, and who wants that? I know I don't. I decided when I was nine years old that only I would determine the direction of my life, and no one else. I assumed that control one evening as I listened to my stepfather walking up the stairs to the bedroom I shared with my younger sister. I vowed right then and there to never be a victim again.

I watch Eli drive down the street and consider the possibility that he may never return. I hope that it's not over, but it's a possibility. I allowed myself to feel too much, and it hurt. It always hurts. I wonder if other people think the way that I do. I don't imagine I'll ever know. At least I can take solace in knowing that Eli was moved by my emotional outburst. He does care, even though he does his best to conceal it. I hear the chirping of insects outside my window. A car parks along Merrin. I watch as a man and woman emerge from the vehicle. The woman walks to the front of the car and waits for the man while looking up at the starlit sky. They hold hands and walk down the sidewalk. I recognize a fleeting bout of jealousy because I doubt I'll ever share a similar experience. Appearances are deceiving most of the time.

I'm lonely. I can still smell Eli. His sweat is still on my skin. I hate being alone. I walk to the kitchen and take a bottle of white wine from the refrigerator. My place is a mess because I haven't been home except to shower, change clothes, and have sex. I laugh to myself when I articulate that thought in my mind. I don't understand why it's considered uncouth for women to have the same thoughts as men. The utensil drawer won't open when I pull on it to retrieve my corkscrew. I push it in and pull it back out again a few times until it opens. I brush my hand over the utensils but can't find the corkscrew. *Damn it.* I need a drink. Frustration builds within me until I want to cry again. I shove the drawer closed with such force that it rattles. I look for something, anything that I can use to open the damn bottle of wine. Crying will only make me feel worse. I grab a butter knife and steady the tip of the blade against the cork and push down with all my might. There's a popping noise. I can see the cork floating on the surface of the wine. I toss the knife on the counter and study the bottle. I take a drink from the bottle and get particles of the cork in my mouth. The wine tastes sweet. I use my forefinger and thumb to rake the tip of my tongue for small parts of the cork. I take another drink and my nerves settle.

Inside the bottom drawer of my bedroom dresser, there is a red envelope that contains a card. I open the drawer and remove the envelope. I run my hand over the handwriting on the front. I trace each letter slowly with my finger before I open the envelope. The card is from the guy I dated for two years after high school. His name was Alex Ketchem. At the bottom of my dresser drawer, I find photographs of us. There's one of us making faces at the camera while resting on the sand at the lake. There's another picture of us kissing in his old rusty Mustang that he loved so much. I think of our last summer together. He's gone now. I miss him terribly.

Alex was the only man in my life who treated me like I was special. He really did love me for me, and not for any other reason. The night before the accident, we drove to a nearby park and sneaked into the woods with the intention of camping outside for the evening. It was summer, and the mosquitos were so thick I could hear them buzzing close to my ear. I planned to give myself to Alex that night, but he told me that we should wait. I remember being confused. Alex told me I should only give myself to him if I loved him. I told him I wasn't sure because I had never been in love, but I thought that I was in love with him. All Alex did was smile and nod his head while saying, "you'll know when you're in love." I didn't know what he meant that night. We spent the rest of that evening getting bitten by mosquitos and sleeping sporadically. Neither of us cared, though. We hugged most of that night to minimize our shivering. I couldn't have known then that the next day a drunk driver would cross the center line and hit Alex's Mustang head-on. The other driver survived, but Alex didn't. I never saw him again. When the police gave me a card in an envelope addressed to me that they had found on his passenger seat, I collapsed, and one of the officers had to catch me before I hit the floor. When I regained consciousness and everyone had left, I opened the letter. I knew then, without any doubt, that I loved him, but it was too late.

I catch myself sniffing as I carefully place the card back into the envelope. I return the envelope to the drawer and look at it one last time before I push the drawer closed. I walk to the bed where I left my phone and check for any messages. There aren't any. An overwhelming fear of abandonment disables me. I feel panicked as I scroll through the contacts on my phone. I push the call button and wait. He answers after the third ring.

"Hello."

"I didn't know who else to call."

"Ryah?"

"Yes. Are you free?"

"When? I'm at work now. Why, what's happening? Are you OK?"

"Not really. I think I'm having some sort of panic attack. Can you come over?"

"When do you want me to visit?"

"Now! I need you now, Bo." There is a pause. "Hello? Are you there?"

"I'm here, Ryah."

"Forget about it. I'm sorry I called."

"I'll be over in ten minutes."

"Are you sure?"

"Yes."

"Thank you…I…I can't breathe very well. I feel like I might pass out."

"Take deep breaths and don't leave the house. I'm on my way."

"Hurry!"

CHAPTER TWENTY
Resigned Wishes

Franki Rose

Everyone tells me I should take it slow with Eli. My mother says it's too soon to get involved with a man again. Even when I explain to her that I've known him since grade school, she doesn't understand. All she can do is talk about Kasey and how crushed I was when we broke up. When I tell her that he has a law degree now and is running Wayside she pauses and then insists that timing is everything. My mother may be right, but I don't care. I can't stop myself. I want to be with Eli.

His knock at the door causes the butterflies in my stomach to intensify so much that I fear I may be unable to speak. I swallow and clear my throat before I open the door and invite him inside. I can smell his cologne as he walks past me to enter my apartment. He is wearing an unbuttoned gray wool jacket over an orange V-neck T-shirt and dark-blue jeans that are worn. I'm so nervous that my hands are shaking.

"I love that shirt," he says as he takes his boots off in the entranceway.

I look down at my plaid pearl-snap shirt and then back at him, surprised he even noticed. In an uneven voice, I reply, "Thank you."

"You're welcome. Well, aren't you going to give me a hug?" He stretches his arms toward me. I hesitate out of shock before I catch myself and walk over to him. I pull him into my body and hold him tightly. His fingertips massage my back. I shiver. When he loosens his grip, I do the same and take a step back. He looks down at me. I look back at him and smile.

I invite him to sit in the living room while I finish preparing the spaghetti dinner.

"Would you like a glass of wine?" I ask as he sits on the couch.

"Yes, please."

"Is red wine OK?"

"That would be great."

I walk into the kitchen and open the bottle of wine with the cork-screw. It makes a pop. I pour a half-full glass and carry it into the living room. I hand it to Eli, who thanks me and takes a drink.

"Dinner should only be a few more minutes. I'm sorry. The bread isn't finished yet."

"Don't apologize. You're too kind. I'm early. There's no rush." He takes another drink of wine. "This wine is good. What kind is it?"

"It's from a winery down south. I went with my mother this past June, and I loved it so much I bought four bottles."

"It's excellent."

"I'm glad you enjoy it. My mother got drunk at the winery and embarrassed me."

Eli laughs. "That sounds like a fun time."

I walk to the kitchen and yell, "You have no idea." I take the bread out of the oven. It is black around the edges. "Shit."

"What?" Eli asks from the living room.

"Oh, nothing."

"Why did you say 'shit' then?"

I take a butter knife and scrape the crust, but the bread is still notice-ably burnt. "I burned the damn bread. I'm sorry."

"It's not a problem, Franki. Really. I'm not hard to please."

"I can only hope that's true."

Eli's laughter from the living room helps me relax.

Eli takes a seat at the table in my kitchen. In the center of the table I have three slender purple candles lit. The flames flicker as I move the bread and the spaghetti to the table. I make Eli's plate and hand it to him. He places it on the table and inspects it with a smile.

"This looks amazing, Franki."

"You may change your mind when you taste it," I say as I fix my own plate. I sit down across from Eli and smile.

Eli asks for a second helping and thanks me again for the meal as I fix his plate and hand it to him. I can't finish my plate. I don't have an appetite. I think I'm too nervous. I refill our glasses with what's left of the wine.

"Would you like me to open another bottle?"

"That's not necessary. I don't want you to waste your favorite wine on me."

"Nonsense." I take the empty bottle to the kitchen and place it on the counter before I open the new bottle and take it back to the table.

Eli finishes his meal and wipes his mouth with his napkin. I take our plates to the kitchen while he finishes his glass of wine. When I return to the table, Eli grabs my hand.

"You're beautiful. Do you know that?" he says in a low voice.

I squeeze his hand. "Thank you."

Eli pulls me to him and kisses me. I can taste the wine on his lips. My eyes open to see that he's looking at me. "I think I like you."

"I like you too," I admit. Eli kisses me again and then blows out the candles.

***

Eli makes me feel like no one I've ever been with. I lay my head on his chest while in bed. I can hear his heart beating. I run fingers over his skin as he caresses my hair.

"Can I see you again?" he asks.

I lift my head from his chest and look at him in the darkness. "Of course you can."

"Good," is all he says before he eases out of bed. I watch as he gets dressed in the darkness. He puts his T-shirt on and pauses. "I have to get home and check on my dad. I'm sorry I can't stay."

I clutch the sheet and hold it against my chest. "I understand," is all I can mutter.

He walks over to me and kisses my forehead. "Thank you for tonight, Franki." He squeezes my hand and then walks out of the bedroom. I hear the front door open and then close. I understand that he can't stay, no matter how much I want him to.

CHAPTER TWENTY-ONE
What She Doesn't Know

Bo Schnep

I kiss Scarlett good night before I leave her house. She has to get to bed early, which works out well enough for me. The porch light is turned off shortly after I start my car. I sit in my parked vehicle for a moment and look through my windshield. I stare into the darkness and feel comforted. Not everything needs to be known.

I'm always coming and going. That's the beauty of my job. It keeps me active and involved enough that people in town don't concern themselves with my personal life. That sounds simple enough, but in a small town, freedom is everything. I arrive at Ryah's a little after eleven in the evening. I'm late on purpose. Ryah has been distant lately. She returns text messages infrequently, and when she does so, it is usually a vague statement followed by a smiley face. I don't appreciate being dismissed. She doesn't think I notice details. She forgets it's my job to be suspicious of people. I know she has a secret. I suppose we all do. Her bedroom light is on. I get out of my car and walk to the front door of her building. I knock on the door and wait. She opens the door and smiles seductively at me. I want to know what she's hiding.

Ryah closes the door and locks it. Nothing about her apartment appears different from any other time I've visited. Two empty wine glasses rest on a coffee table next to a bowl with a fork handle sticking out. Magazines cover the floor by her chair, and some shirts are draped over her small couch.

"I'm sorry about the mess," she says after noticing me looking around.

"I don't care. You know that." I turn around just as Ryah throws her arms around me and pushes me against the wall. She kisses me passionately, and when I recover enough to kiss her back, she pulls away. "What was that for?"

She offers a girlish grin. "I like you."

"I like you too." Ryah walks past me into the living room. I watch her before I realize that I am no longer in control. She's wearing very short orange cotton shorts and a thin white tank top without a bra. Ryah stops in the middle of the living room and turns around to face me. She looks me over deliberately and then smirks. I can't talk.

"Are you coming?" she asks. I don't answer. I have to have her in that moment. I walk to her and grip her upper arm. I can feel her resist just enough that I wrap my other arm around her waist. She looks up at me. No matter how much she wants me to believe she's innocent and pure, I know she's not. I kiss her on the lips and she pulls away. I try again. She pulls away. I grab her hair and hold her head still. I kiss her, and this time she responds. Her body goes limp and she is mine.

***

Ryah takes a shower after we're finished, as I lie in bed with the television on. I'm not watching it. I can't focus. I don't understand Ryah. *Is she incapable of genuine feelings?* Maybe someone hurt her. *Should I ask her?* I hear my phone vibrate and get out of bed to look for my pants. I find them in the corner of the room next to a pile of Ryah's laundry. I check it and see a text from Scarlett that says, "I can't sleep."

I type back, "What's wrong?"

I walk back to the bed and lie down. Scarlett replies immediately with, "I don't know."

I send, "I'm sorry."

The shower stops. Another message from Scarlett says, "Will you come over?"

I send, "Now?"

She responds, "Yes."

Ryah opens the bathroom door. Steam pours into the bedroom. She stands naked in the doorway while drying her hair. "You're always on your phone," she teases.

"Work beckons."

"What is it now? Can't you tell them that you're busy?"

"I can't lie to my boss."

"It's not so difficult." Ryah walks over to the bed and kisses me. "Are you sure you can't stay?"

"I really need to go." I feel my cell phone vibrate. "See?" I say, knowing she heard the sound of the incoming message.

She backs away. "Fine."

I check my phone to see a text from Scarlett that reads, "?" I begin to type a reply to Scarlett and quickly exit it as Ryah walks toward me again.

"You're going to stay with me," Ryah commands. "I won't take no for an answer." I set my phone on the floor beside the bed and pull Ryah by her wrist until she collapses on top of me. Her skin is still warm from the shower. I kiss her. "You will stay, won't you?"

I hear my phone vibrate.

CHAPTER TWENTY-TWO
Shared Past

Kasey Price

I feel guilty because I was caught. That's the honest truth. Guilt only exists when someone else notices our sins. I shouldn't have wanted her like I did. But for some reason, I had to know what it was like to be with someone like her. Maybe it's because she is the type of girl who never paid attention to someone like me. I obsessed about her body and how it would feel against mine. I had to know. After it happened, I felt unfulfilled. I don't know how Franki suspected anything. She never told me why she believed I had been with Ryah. My mind worked over all the possibilities. There's no way Ryah would've told Franki. Perhaps Franki could sense the change somehow. If I could do it all over again, I'm still not sure I could resist Ryah. But I know if I had a second chance, I wouldn't get caught.

"I'm seeing someone," Franki confirms. She's still wearing her pink work polo shirt with blank pants that are wrinkled. Her hair is pulled back into a ponytail except for a strand that she keeps securing behind her ear. She looks tired but cute.

"Who is it?"

Franki looks away. "I don't want to say."

"Why not?"

"Because it doesn't matter." She checks her hands in a nervous way.

I step toward her so she looks at me. "It matters to me."

Franki steps back. "Kasey, we are over. We've talked about this."

"Does that mean we can't be friends?"

"I never said that."

"Well you're not acting very friendly. I'm not going to flip out or anything. I want to know who has replaced me."

"Quit antagonizing me, Kasey. Nobody has replaced you. I need to move on. You need to move on. It's that simple." She takes a deep breath.

"I understand. I thought…oh, never mind."

"I'm sorry." Franki looks at me with sad eyes.

"There's nothing that can be done now," I say in a flat tone. "Maybe we can become friends. Do you think that's possible?"

Franki smiles. "I would like that."

"Me too." Franki reaches for me and hugs me. I hug her back and squeeze her. Her scent causes my stomach to feel sick. I remember being happy once.

I leave Franki's house and drive to Ryah's apartment. I see her car parked along the street and decide to visit her. I knock on her door. She answers in the outfit she must have worn to work. Her hair has been curled so that it spirals down her back, and her skirt is just long enough that it passes for appropriate attire. Her blouse is unbuttoned so that her cleavage is showing.

"Kasey, come in." I walk inside her apartment and smell some kind of stir-fry cooking. "I'm in the middle of fixing dinner. I wasn't expecting you. Would you like to stay and eat? I should have enough."

"I'm not really hungry."

"It's past six. You're here; you might as well eat something. Give me a few minutes to finish cooking." Ryah walks to the kitchen, and I hear the stir-fry sizzling. "Come in here and talk to me," she yells.

I walk to the kitchen and stand in the entranceway. Ryah is digging at the rice with a wooden spatula as steam clouds the room.

"I don't mean to bother you. I guess I felt like seeing a friendly face."

Ryah turns her head to face me. "Is something wrong?" She turns the stove off and moves the pan to a hot pad to cool while she gets two plates out of her cabinet.

"I don't know. Maybe. Probably not. How are you?"

Ryah looks at me, noticeably confused. "I'm OK," she says while filling two glasses with filtered water from the refrigerator. "Why do you ask?"

"I haven't heard from you. I know you needed space, so I didn't want to bother you, but I miss talking to you." I see Ryah smile to herself as she spoons stir-fry onto two white porcelain plates. "I hope that's OK to say."

"Of course it's OK to say. I miss you too. She walks past me into the small dining area and sets the plates on the tiny metal table. "Could you grab our drinks?"

I use my fork to move the rice on my plate around, but I don't take a bite. I watch Ryah eat. Her femininity is attractive to me. She enjoys being a woman. I take a drink of water.

"You have to eat, Kasey. Don't be shy. We're friends, remember?"

"I had hoped that hadn't changed." I poke at the rice and steak chunks on my plate and finally take a small bite. It's spicy but good.

Ryah pulls her fork from her mouth. "Don't be silly. I'm actually glad you visited. I have been meaning to call you."

I take another drink of water. "Oh yeah? Any reason?"

Ryah clears her throat. "Franki."

"What about Franki?"

"She asked me about you."

I take a deep breath. "What about me?"

"Well, she asked if we ever talked."

"When did she ask you this?"

"Recently. I thought she had moved on, but apparently not." Ryah takes a drink and looks at me intently before she resumes eating.

"She told me she has moved on. I don't know why she would still ask about you and me."

"I don't know. I thought you should be aware, though. There's still some part of her that can't give up. I only tell you so you can be careful." I look at Ryah. She never appears to be bothered, though I know she is the one who needs to be careful.

"Thank you for the warning," I say so that she thinks she has nothing to worry about.

Ryah wipes her mouth with her napkin. "Don't mention it. Is there anything else new with you?"

"Not too much. How about you?"

"Same old life here. Nothing changes much in this town."

"I guess you're right. The town stays the same. It's the people who change."

Ryah giggles. "I think you're right about that, Kasey. I hadn't thought of it that way." Ryah takes a drink of water while still smirking. "Can you stay for a little while longer?"

"I don't know if that's a good idea."

She offers a mischievous grin. "Why not? Can't old friends catch up without everyone in town getting the wrong idea?"

I laugh. "You're a bad girl. You do know that, right?"

"Am I?"

CHAPTER TWENTY-THREE

He Can't Save Me

Ryah Klein

Falling in love is the easy part. Staying in love is what's so difficult. I can't understand how people can stay with just one person. Not that I'm opposed to the idea, but it seems to be more fantasy than anything else. I guess I struggle with trust. I think the problem I have with trust is that it represents the misguided belief that other people are in some way better than I am. *How can I trust someone when I can't trust myself?*

No matter how hard I try, I can't break Eli's resolve. I'm not sure if he is playing a game with me or if he doesn't care. His lack of interest makes me think about him more than I like to admit. There has to be something to him other than an uncaring person motivated by self-interest. Deep beneath the surface, there must be emotions that have been buried for too long. I want to believe I can make him feel again, but I'm losing faith.

Bo walks to the kitchen and pours a glass of water. He walks back to the bedroom and sits on the edge of the bed. I watch him drink the water. His muscled torso looks perfect. The mask of perfection is what causes the disdain I feel. It conceals what isn't there. He looks over his shoulder at me. I feel very little. *When will the masquerade end?*

Bo makes up an excuse to explain why he has to leave. I don't have the energy to question him. I let him go. Everyone leaves eventually. I've gotten used to it over the years. I don't bother to get out of bed. I pull the sheet over me and feel the soft cotton against my naked body. The summer is over now, and as a result, a part of me feels less alive. I stare out the window at the dark-blue sky. *Does my life matter?*

My phone doesn't ring. All I'm left with are the sounds of cars passing and birds chirping outside my window. Life happens regardless, but on days like this, I don't bother to get out of bed to experience it. I need to find someone who cares. If I can't find him, then someone new will do. I want something different and I won't feel alive until I find it.

I hear someone knock on the front door but I don't budge. The knock sounds again. I roll over in bed and hope the knocking stops. A third knock sounds. I kick the sheets off and put on a blue button-down dress shirt Bo left two nights ago when he received a message and had to run off to God knows where to do God knows what. I button the two middle buttons as I walk to answer the door. A fourth knock sounds, and I yell, "Wait a second, I'm coming!"

I open the door and find myself paralyzed with disbelief. My stomach drops. I can't speak. It's him. I can't believe it. It's really him. He looks at me and smiles casually.

"Can I come in, Ryah?"

I can't move. I want to wrap my arms around him and pull him close to me while kissing his lips. I want him to feel how much I've missed him. If only I could whisper in his ear how much I need him and how he could save me from myself. Instead, all I say is, "Sure."

Eli walks past me and stands in the living room. His long-sleeve T-shirt is untucked and his blue jeans hang lower than usual without a belt.

"How are you, Ryah?"

I close the front door and stare at him. My heart beats faster. I want him to know every part of me. "Where have you been?"

"What do you mean?" He turns to inspect my living room. "I see not much has changed."

"I haven't heard from you in a while. I thought...forget it."

Eli lifts a magazine from my coffee table and looks at the cover before tossing it back down. "You thought what?"

"Don't worry about it."

He walks toward me and gently grabs my upper arms with his hands. "I want to know."

"I thought you would text me, or call me, or something. I guess...I'm being stupid."

Eli's eyes peer into mine. "You're not being stupid. Don't say that."

"It's how I feel." I can't move. I hope he pulls me closer to him.

"You shouldn't feel that way. I've been busy. There's been a lot going on with Wayside and my dad. It has nothing to do with you. You know that, right?"

I look at Eli. He is difficult to read. "I want to believe you."

"You should believe me, Ryah." Eli pulls me into him and hugs me. I want to make him work harder for my affection, but my arms gradually wrap around him, and suddenly I am holding him against me and gripping the back of his shirt. I hate how weak I am.

A moment of tenderness leads to an evening of passion. There is desperation in the way he kisses me, the way he pulls my hair, and the way he holds my naked body against his after it's over. Neither of us can speak. Our breathing is heavy and uneven. He stays on top of me. I can feel his body gradually relax. He rolls off me and lies next to me. I stare at the ceiling and wish I could say something meaningful.

"You're amazing, Ryah," he says between pants.

I turn my head and look at him. His skin glistens with sweat. "I think we fit well together."

"I would have to agree." He wipes his forehead with the back of his hand. I watch him and want him to never leave. He gets out of bed.

"Where are you going?" I ask. "I want you to stay."

"I need a drink. Do you want one?"

"Sure. Can you stay tonight?" I ask. I sound so pathetic.

"Is that what you want?"

CHAPTER TWENTY-FOUR

Boxes in the Closet

Scarlett Davison

C an lovers be too damaged to love? I feel like some people have been hurt so badly that it's impossible to ever reclaim who they once were. I feel this way. I want to believe that love can heal us even when it feels like all it has done is cause pain. The cinnamon candles I lit an hour ago fill my house with an aroma that reminds me of happier times. I pour a cup of coffee and blow into the mug before taking a drink. It's unusually cool for early September. It has been drizzling off and on all afternoon. I look out the window in my living room at the overcast sky, which provides no hope for sunlight. I take another drink of coffee and feel its warmth settle in my stomach. I have nothing to do but sit and think about the past. I can hear the rain start again. My house makes me feel lonely sometimes. *Should I have moved to Payne?* I hate second-guessing myself.

I walk into the spare bedroom and sit on the small bed by the window and listen to the rain patter against the glass. The rhythmic sound soothes me as I stare at the closet door. I know I shouldn't open the closet, but I want to. The cardboard boxes inside have remained sealed shut since he left. There is a reason I have placed them out of view. I want to forget about the contents of those boxes just like I want to forget about him, but no matter how much I try, I can't forget. My memories are too vivid and the emotions are too real. I walk to the closet and stop at the door. I take a deep breath. His last words to me will still sting when I think of them. He will still be gone and I will still be alone. I open the door and see the boxes stacked on one another. Sifting through those objects won't make me feel any better.

The boxes are labeled "memories" with black permanent marker. I lift the top one off the stack and place it on the floor. I pull the folded cardboard apart to open the box, and the first item I see is a silly tack board we made that is covered with pictures of us together and little notes we wrote to each other. I read a note he wrote to me on a small piece of paper that says, "I love you." He left it on his pillow so I would find it the morning of my last final my senior year in college. The picture beside the note is a close-up photograph we took of ourselves, smiling at my parents' place in the country. Next to that picture is a yellow sticky note that reads, "dork," with an arrow pointing at me. I laugh.

The next box has a few shirts that belonged to him. He never bothered to pick them up. I told myself I would keep them in case he wanted them later, but I really kept them because I couldn't bring myself to let them go. I unfold the green concert T-shirt with tiny holes in the shoulder and sleeve. No matter how many times I told him to throw the old shirt away because it was faded and the material had thinned, he wouldn't. He used to insist it was his favorite shirt. I put the shirt to my face. His scent has faded. I fold it again and put it back in the box on top of his old work jeans.

The final box contains photo albums I made for him as gifts for every Christmas we shared. Each page has pictures and girly notes written in glitter that I did because I knew he would say it was annoying, even though I could tell he thought it was cute. I flip through them and remember our trip to Chicago, when we stayed in a hotel together for the first time. He treated me so well that night. We got drunk on cheap wine he stole from his father and did ballroom dances around room without any music. From our balcony, the world looked like it was created just for us. He told me he loved me that night as we looked at the glowing city skyline.

I found the last note he ever wrote to me in the bottom of the box. He wrote it the night he found out what I had done. It says, "No matter what, I will always love you." I read it a few times. If only he had meant it. I leave the note on the floor as I pack the boxes and fold them closed. I turn to pick up the first box and kick my coffee mug with my foot. I pull my foot back when I realize that the remnants of my coffee have covered the note on the floor. My heart stops. I drop to the floor and lift the note, but it's drenched and stained brown. I run frantically to the bathroom with the note pinched between my forefinger and thumb. I put the soggy paper on the edge of the sink and use a towel to dab the note dry. The ink is smudged. I feel sick to my stomach. I can't breathe. I dab it over and over, but the words are barely legible. My vision blurs as tears roll down my cheeks and drip from my chin. I pound the sink counter with my closed fist and collapse on the bathroom floor.

I made mistakes. God knows I did. But I don't deserve this. I don't deserve to be forgotten. I shared parts of me with him that I had never shared with another person, and now the letter is gone. It only reminds me that he is gone. I would give anything to see him smile at me again and to know that I caused his happiness. *Why can't he love me the way I love him? Why did he leave me when I needed him the most? Why couldn't he accept that it wasn't the right time for either of us?* I did it for him, not me.

CHAPTER TWENTY-FIVE
All of Myself

Elijah Noor

A genuine emotion feels like a fire that must be contained. Years of hurt will teach anyone that lesson. I pour a cup of coffee and listen to the sad music playing in the background. No matter how much I've tried to recover, the hurt still lingers. At times I still obsess over the happiness I once felt and how everything ended so abruptly. I still can't believe she did that to me. He would have been almost two years old by now had it all happened differently. Maybe it shouldn't bother me any longer. I hear my phone sound with an incoming text from Franki that reads, "Do you want to meet me after work?" I don't respond. After I finish my coffee, I finish getting dressed. I refuse to be hurt again.

I drive past the coffee shop where Franki works. I consider stopping for a moment but decide doing so wouldn't make me feel any better. I don't want to be the one who shows her love isn't real, even though it would be better for her if she knew. I park in the lot behind Wayside and enter through the back door of the building. I walk to the bar to find my servers doing the inventory. They ask me a few questions about supplies, and I answer them. I walk to the kitchen to talk to my father.

"There he is," he says when he sees me approaching.

I smile. "I'm here."

"Fifteen minutes late, as usual. How many times must I explain the importance of punctuality?" He's irritated with me. I'm used to it.

"Yeah, yeah," I reply. He waves his hand to dismiss my response as I walk to his office. I sit down and turn on the computer. I hear footsteps and look up to see my father standing in the doorway.

"Are you going to order a new keg? What about those empty bottles of liquor? I told you I wanted that done last week."

I turn from the computer and look at him. "I am going to make the order as soon as the entire inventory is taken. I told you that it doesn't make sense to make more than one order and pay more in delivery costs. I'm trying to save you some money. You do want me to save you money, don't you?"

He heaves a sigh. "Don't give me any shit. Just get it done."

"Consider it done," I say while staring into his eyes. I can feel my heart beating faster, despite my calm demeanor.

"Good. Are you OK? You haven't stopped by." His voice is softer now. He is the master of manipulation.

"I'm well. I've been busy, is all. I should be asking you that question." I notice that he looks pale as he leans against the doorway

"I feel fine. You need to quit chasing all the girls in this town. What happened to you settling down? I didn't worry about you when you were with—"

I interrupt him. "Don't start with that shit, Dad. I don't want to hear it. You can't believe everything people in this town say."

He rolls his eyes. "I hear quite a bit about you. You need to find a good woman. You're not in college any longer. There are good women out there, but you're not going to meet them in a bar."

"Where are they then? Church?"

"It wouldn't hurt you to attend Mass. God has a plan for you, you know."

"I'm not going to Mass, Dad. I don't need a woman to be happy." I turn to face the computer and open the inventory documents.

He stands motionless for a moment. "I know your last relationship ended with a lot of heartache, Eli. But that's no reason to give up. The right person is out there for you. You have to trust that."

"I trust very little," I say without looking away from the computer screen.

"That's a shame. You have a lot to offer, but you can't spend the rest of your life sulking because of one failed relationship. You have to move on." I keep typing without responding. "Think about it," he says. He leaves the office. I pick up the phone and place the order. I know what I'm doing.

I leave Wayside and walk to the coffee shop where Franki works. Franki sees me enter the shop and smiles at me. I wave as I approach the counter.

"Eli, it's great to see you. What a surprise. Can I get you something?"

I look at their menu even though I know what I want. "I'll have a black coffee to go." Franki types the order into the register and I pay her the dollar and a quarter. While she pours the coffee, I tap my finger on the counter and look around the shop at the patrons. I recognize everyone in the shop. I offer a friendly smile to those who make eye contact with me.

"Here you go. Did you get my text?" Franki asks as she hands me my coffee in a to-go cup.

"Oh, yeah. I'm sorry I didn't respond. I had to get to Wayside. My father was giving me hell because I was late."

"Oh no. What did he say?"

"The same old bullshit about me not taking my responsibilities seriously and how I need to settle down and return to church. He still thinks everything he hears about me is true." I pull a few napkins from the dispenser even though I don't need them. I stuff them into my pocket. Sometimes I do meaningless things to distract myself from the realization that there is no special meaning woven into the fabric of existence. I might as well be entertained.

"I'm sure you said something sarcastic that made him regret that speech." Franki laughs. I do too. A customer enters the store and stands behind me.

"I better let you get back to work. Talk to me later?"

"Sure! I'll text you after work."

I take a sip from my coffee and tap the counter with my finger before I turn around and leave.

CHAPTER TWENTY-SIX
Something is Wrong

Franki Rose

I don't understand him. He says to text him or call him, and then he doesn't respond. *Is this all a game to Eli?* I worry that maybe I care too much and that maybe he doesn't care at all. No matter what, I have to maintain hope. Without hope, I have nothing. I text him again and look out the window in my living room. Orange streaks paint the sky as the sun sets. I want to share my life with someone special. Sometimes I think that's too much to ask.

I turn the television on and stare at the screen. I hear the noise and see the images, but my brain doesn't process the information. I can't focus on anything. I feel detached from everyone in my life. It's been so long since I felt normal. Credits appear on my television. I don't even know what show I just watched, but it's over now. I hope my life doesn't end the same way.

Another show starts. I concentrate enough to see a commercial where a stained T-shirt is dipped into a bowl of cleaning solution, and when it is withdrawn from the liquid, the stain is no longer detectable. People will believe anything they see. My cell phone vibrates on the arm of my chair. I look down to see it's my mother calling. I let it ring. After five rings, the sound stops. The screen displays a new voice mail message. I want to tell my mother how hollow I feel, but she won't understand. She thinks guys are decent and trustworthy.

The darkness reminds me I'm alone. Another program on the television sounds in the background, but I'm not really paying attention. It's some makeover show. I think about changing it. The same stain removal commercial plays. My phone sounds again. It's my mother. I don't want to talk to her, but after the fourth ring, I decide to answer.

"Hello," I say in a monotone.

"Franki, what are you doing? I just called. Are you busy?"

I roll my eyes and groan audibly into the phone. "I'm not doing anything. What's going on?"

"Are you sure I'm not bothering you? You're not on a date, are you?"

"No, I'm not on a date, but thanks for making me feel even more pathetic about sitting in my house alone watching shitty television."

"Franki!" she gasps.

"I'm sorry, Mom. I've had a bad night," I say, feeling a bit embarrassed that I used profanity.

"What's wrong, Franki? You're too young to be sitting in your house feeling sorry for yourself."

"I know. That's what's wrong. I should be out doing something, but instead I'm here doing nothing. I'm not even watching the shit—I mean, crappy television show."

She pauses but seems pleased I corrected myself. "Then why are you doing it?"

"I don't know. I guess I'm upset."

"Did something happen?"

"No. Not really. Eli didn't call, and he said that he would."

"Maybe he got busy. Doesn't he run that one restaurant in town?"

"Wayside. He manages Wayside. Maybe you're right. I don't know. It hurts when he says he'll call and then he doesn't." I clear my throat after I finish.

"You shouldn't wait on him, Franki. You're a pretty girl. Make him chase you. Don't make yourself so available. Men don't find that attractive. They want a challenge." I hear the rustling of papers. I wonder what she is doing that is so important that she can't devote her full attention to me.

"That's the problem. I don't want to wait on him. I don't know. I don't want anyone else, though, if that makes sense."

"Oh." A pause follows, and the papers stop shuffling. A sudden sadness grips me and my eyes tear up. "Are you in love with him?" she asks hesitantly.

"No. I don't think so. I haven't dated him very long. I can't describe it." I swallow and feign a cough so that she doesn't hear my voice crack.

"Franki, don't let Eli wear you down like Kasey did. I don't want you to ever be that sad again."

"Kasey didn't wear me down. It was the situation that made me so sad. The dishonesty is difficult to understand."

"Whose dishonesty?"

"Everyone's."

My mother says she has to go, and I don't try to stop her. I hang up and stare at the television. The same commercial plays. I watch it again. I don't want to be alone. I text Kasey, "What are you doing?"

Within the first minute he replies, "Nothing, what's up?"

I think for a moment. I wish Eli would call. I text Kasey, "Do you want to come over?" I can feel my heart beating in my chest. I look away from my phone. I want to feel less desperate. I start thinking of what I'll tell Kasey later if he doesn't respond tonight. I could tell him that I was going to set him up with a friend but that she backed out at the last second. I could tell him that I was drunk with friends and that I was messing with him. Or I could tell him that I miss him and feel lonely without him around. Nobody wants to hear the truth, though. My phone vibrates. I refrain from checking it right away. Even though I am by myself, I don't want to admit that I'm overly anxious to see his response.

When I open his text message, it reads, "I'll be there in ten minutes." I feel relief momentarily, followed by dread.

Kasey arrives and knocks on my front door. I want him to leave. I consider not answering the door, but do so after he knocks a second time.

"Are you OK?" he asks as soon as I open the door.

"Yes, I'm fine. Why?"

"Uh, because I don't hear from you ever anymore and all of a sudden you're inviting me over to your house late at night."

"I had a bad day is all. Come in." Kasey walks past me and I close the front door. I turn around to find him staring at me. "What?"

"Nothing."

"Would you like something to drink? I have a few light beers left, I think."

"That would be fine." I walk to the kitchen to get one. I pause by the refrigerator to compose myself. I don't want Kasey to know I'm upset. "What the hell are you watching?" he yells from the living room.

"You can change it. I wasn't watching anything. I just had it on."

I return from the kitchen and hand Kasey a beer. "Are you not having one?" he asks.

"No. I don't feel like drinking tonight."

I sit in the chair next to the couch where Kasey sits. "What are you doing over there?" he asks after taking a drink.

"What do you mean?"

"Sit next to me." I tilt my head and look at him accusingly. "Come on. You asked me over here, and I came, didn't I?"

I smile. Kasey is sweet sometimes.

I stand up slowly and walk to him. The black shorts I have on don't conceal much, and I don't want Kasey to look at me, but when he does, it feels familiar. I sit next to him, and he puts his arm around me and hugs me. I pat his arm with my hand. "Oh, come on. You can at least give me a good hug." He sets his beer on the end table. I reach to hug him, and when I do so, his touch causes me to ease into the embrace. He holds me tightly, and I feel a tad lighter.

"Thank you."

"You don't have to thank me," he says.

"I don't know what to think anymore."

"Don't take this the wrong way, Franki, but sometimes you think too much."

"What do you mean?"

Kasey leans forward and kisses me on the lips. I turn my head just after his lips touch mine. "What are you doing?"

"You're thinking, not feeling."

He moves close again. "We can't!" I warn him.

"Why not?" He looks into my eyes and kisses me. This time I don't turn away.

CHAPTER TWENTY-SEVEN
True Friends

Bo Schnep

"**C**alm down, what's the problem?" I ask.

"Can you get here? It's Ryah." Eli's voice sounds agitated on the phone.

"Where is she? What's going on?"

"She's here at Wayside. She's drunk as hell and starting to make a scene. I want someone I can trust to take her home."

"Don't let her leave. I'll be right there."

"Hurry," Eli urges before he hangs up. I put my phone in my front pants pocket and grab the black wool blazer I wore to work today. I speed to the bar. The whole way there I think about what to expect when I arrive. *Why is Ryah upset?*

I enter through the back door and find Ryah sitting at the end of the bar with red eyes. She glares at me with contempt as I approach her.

"What's wrong?" I ask, reaching for her arm.

"Nothing. Why are you here?" she asks. Her words are noticeably slurred.

"Are you OK?"

"Yes, why wouldn't I be?" Ryah takes a drink from a bottle of beer.

Eli motions for me to walk to the other side of the bar.

"Thanks for coming. I'm sorry to call you so late, but I didn't know who else could help," he says in low voice.

"What's going on?"

"She's drunk and started to cause a scene because I wouldn't serve her any longer. She calmed down when I gave her a beer. I want to make sure she has a safe ride home."

"Damn, Eli. You scared the shit out of me. I thought something serious happened."

"Oh, no. I apologize. She started to yell at me, and I called you. I didn't know who else would be able to handle this situation with discretion. I don't want Ryah to face any consequences for a night she'll likely forget."

I take a deep breath. "You did the right thing. You're right. There's no reason for Ryah to get herself into any trouble. Let me go speak to her again."

"Be careful. She's pissed off for some reason. She almost bit my head off for refusing to serve her." Eli laughs.

"I had plenty of practice dealing with belligerent drunks my first few years on the force. I'll handle her as gently as I can."

Eli extends his hand to me and we shake. "Thanks, Bo. I owe you for this one. You're a good friend."

"Don't worry about it, Eli. Tomorrow it will be like this never happened." Eli nods his head and smiles. I walk toward Ryah again. Tears are rolling down her cheeks, but she's not sobbing. She looks even more intoxicated than when I initially saw her.

"Come on, Ryah."

"What?" she asks, confused.

"Let's go. I'm here to take you home." I stand beside her.

"I'm not leaving," she states defiantly.

"Ryah, you're drunk. Let's get you home so you can sleep this off. It's not a big deal; it's just time to go."

"Says who?"

"Come on, Ryah. Don't act like this. I want to help you."

"You don't want to help me. I've done nothing wrong, Bo. So leave me alone. I don't want to go home."

"Ryah, please. Don't make a scene."

"Don't tell me what to do! I'm not leaving."

"Eli asked that you leave. He's being very kind about all of this. He's not angry; he called me to make sure you get home safely."

"Oh really? Eli said that he wanted me to leave? Well, why don't you tell that asshole to come over here and tell me to leave? Who does he think he is, calling you? And what does that make you? His servant?"

"Ryah, stop!" I demand. "You can either accept a ride from me or you can take your chances with a uniformed police officer when Eli calls to have you removed. Trust me, this is not worth a night in jail. Will you trust me?"

"Trust is a form of masochism."

"Come on," I urge as I place a hand on her forearm. She pulls away but doesn't resist when I place my hand on her arm a second time.

"OK. OK! I'll go with you, but don't say Eli is kind. Nothing about Eli is kind. He's an asshole. You got that? He's the worst person I have ever known, and I've known some bad people in my life." She stands, and I guide her to make sure she doesn't fall over.

"Don't say that. Eli is my friend," I tell her.

Ryah turns to look at Eli, who is stationed behind the bar. His face remains expressionless. "Is that what you think? Do you really think he's your friend?"

CHAPTER TWENTY-EIGHT
I'm Cold

Ryah Klein

I wake up shivering in just my panties. I sit up in bed. My vision blurs with the worst headache I have ever experienced. *What happened last night?* I rub my eyes and try to piece together the bits of memory that remain. I remember going to Wayside to see Eli and having a few too many rum and Diet Cokes. Then Bo arrived. I look at the digital clock on my bedside table and panic until I remember that it's Saturday and I don't have to work. I close my eyes and rub my temples with my index fingers. *Who brought me home last night?*

I see a piece of paper on the windshield of my car. My head hurts too badly to go outside immediately and inspect it. Instead, I drink my coffee and watch the paper flap in the breeze. I feel sick. I walk to the bathroom, where I find my phone and keys in the front pocket of my jeans, which are on the floor beside the bathtub, for some reason. My phone is dead, so I can't check my messages. My head hurts so badly that I kneel in front of the toilet in case I get sick. I dry heave a few times and then feel the nausea subside. I move to the sink. I turn the faucet on and cup my hands together. I relish the cold sensation as the water pools in my palms. I splash my face once, and then a second time before I look at myself in the mirror. I watch the drops of water fall from my eyelashes as I use my fingertips to wipe the clumpy mascara off my eyelids. My hair smells like smoke and is tangled enough that I don't bother trying to run my fingers through the mess. I look tired. Twenty-eight is a difficult age.

When my phone has enough of a charge that it turns on, I check my messages. There are six missed text messages and two missed calls, all from Bo. The text messages explain that he picked me up from the bar and drove me home. One details how difficult I am, followed by the final one that says he made sure to lay me on my stomach before leaving. The two missed calls are from today, but there is no voice mail message. I type a text to Bo that says, "I survived. Thanks!" He responds within a few minutes, but I don't answer. I'm too sick to feel any obligation to engage in pleasantries. Bo perceives my neglect as discomfort at first and sends me a barrage of text messages asking if I'm OK, followed by questions about whether or not I'm mad at him. I finally send him another text that says, "I'm sick, but OK. There's no reason to be mad at you. Everything is fine."

Bo sends me three quick text messages in response. I glance at the first two, but the third gets my attention. It states, "I thought you might get angry at me since Eli called me to pick you up from the bar. Don't worry. He didn't suspect anything." Rage builds within me. I throw my phone to the floor and pace from one side of the room to the other. *Eli called Bo? Why would he do that? Does Eli know more than he is revealing? Did I just fuck up my chances with the only man I really want?* I want to scream. I pace back and forth until I glance out the window again. I stop moving and study the paper secured under the windshield wiper of my car as it stirs in the wind.

I put on a T-shirt and pair of shorts that don't match and rush out of my apartment to investigate the paper. I can see there is writing on it and quickly pluck the note from the windshield. It reads, "Don't hate me." There's no signature, and I don't recognize the handwriting. *Who doesn't want me to hate them? What happened last night?* I check the back of the paper and then reread the message. I try to think who would go to the effort of putting a note on the windshield of my car in the middle of the night. Bo would have no reason to. He sent text messages and even called in an attempt to determine my mood. Maybe Kasey visited, and when I didn't respond, he immediately assumed that I was back to ignoring him. He can be so needy. I look at the note again, as if somehow my questions will be answered if I study it more intently. I look around my car, but I can't find anything else out of the ordinary. A middle-aged man walks by on the sidewalk. His leashed dog stops and pisses on the lawn. I watch but don't say anything. He waits until his dog finishes, and then he tugs on the leash and they walk away.

CHAPTER TWENTY-NINE
Same Actions, Different People

Scarlett Davison

I know Bo is cheating on me. I suspected something wasn't right beforehand, but last evening when he left in the middle of the night, I knew. I watched him walk out of the bedroom, and when he turned around to see if I was awake, I kept my eyes open so he could see that I was. He didn't say anything.

His text messages are short and purposely vague. They are the sure sign that he feels guilty and wants to determine if he has been too transparent. I don't reply right away. I want him to suffer a bit. I'm not sure why, but I'm not too upset about it. I guess I expected that Bo wouldn't be faithful. It's not whether or not people lie. Everyone lies. The question is whether or not you choose to believe the lie. I don't know what I believe anymore.

Bo arrives at my place right after work. He is still wearing his white button-down dress shirt and his black dress pants that are creased perfectly. His standard black blazer fits well and accentuates his thin physique. When I see him, I want to mess up his blond curls.

"Hey, Scarlett, I'm sorry I'm late. I had to run by the office on my way here. You look great." I know he's aware that something is awry, because his compliment is unwarranted. I do not look great. My jeans are old and my pale arms look terrible. I should have put on a different shirt to hide them.

"Thank you. How was your day?" I ask.

His eyes study me quickly before he busies himself by untucking his shirt. He sighs. "It was a long day. Did you do anything exciting on your day off?"

I walk back to the kitchen to finish preparing the chicken. Bo follows me into the kitchen, where he stands and unbuttons his shirt. He looks good. He always looks good. "I didn't do too much, really. I was hoping you wouldn't have to leave during the night again," I say casually.

Bo scratches his head. "I know. I'm sorry about that. I hate getting called in at night, especially if I'm with you."

"It's part of the job. I understand."

Bo looks at me and then looks at the plates I have on the counter. "Do you need any help in here?"

I know Bo doesn't want to help. He has never helped with dinner. "No. Dinner is almost done. Grab yourself a beer if you'd like and relax."

Bo opens the refrigerator and grabs a bottle of beer. He twists the cap off and throws it in the trash can. Just as he's walking out of the kitchen, he stops in the doorway and says, "You're the best, Scarlett. You really are."

Through the whole dinner, I sit and listen to Bo talk about his day. I don't know what is true and what isn't, and as a result, I lose interest. I just sit and periodically nod, which seems to pacify Bo. He keeps right on talking. I think about his departure last night and where he really went. I imagine him meeting whoever the other girl is and having my scent still on him. I wonder if he even feels the slightest bit of remorse. I wonder if anyone feels remorse.

I allow Bo to stay the night. My weakness is inescapable. He lies next to me with his right arm draped over my stomach. I can hear his breathing. He twitches a few times, and then he's still. I watch him sleep for a few minutes. I want to sleep too, but I can't. Instead I stare at the ceiling and consider what I want. I know I want a real relationship. I want to feel beautiful again. I want to experience real emotions like I used to before everything changed. I want something I don't have, but I'm too afraid to abandon what I *do* have. Whenever Bo awakes, I know I'll watch him get dressed and hope the entire time that he stays with me just so I'm not alone.

CHAPTER THIRTY
They're All Strangers

Elijah Noor

How am I supposed to act? The whole town is here, and everyone is staring at me to see what I'm going to do. All I can do is stand by myself and nod as people pass by me. Person after person expresses condolences as I mutter, "Thank you." My father is dead. Everything in my life has suddenly changed. All I want to do is go home and be alone. Sometimes the best of intentions only cause more misery.

Franki volunteered to organize the meal after my father's viewing. I decided to close the restaurant to patrons and offer an invitation to anyone who wanted to gather to discuss their favorite memories of my father. He would have enjoyed that. To minimize time and costs, Franki suggested that I offer appetizers and beer. Surprisingly, many of Dad's friends offered to help do the cooking and bartending. Franki took care of the rest. She really is great.

I walk from one group of people to the next. Everyone has a memory of my father they want to share. I know almost none of the stories they tell. I listen and then smile or laugh before moving on to the next group of people calling my name. I recognize most of the people, but I don't feel connected to any of them. I excuse myself and walk to the kitchen, where I stop to gather myself. I watch people moving in and out of the kitchen. My father is gone. None of this matters.

Franki finds me sitting in my office with the lights off.

"Are you OK?" she asks with trepidation in her voice.

I lift my head to look at her as she stands in the doorway. The light behind her casts a dreamy silhouette. "I'm fine. Thanks for asking."

Franki clears her throat. She's noticeably nervous. "Why don't you come out here? You don't have to talk to anyone, but being around other people who love your father may help."

I look down at some of the papers on my desk. I notice one that has my father's signature on it. "I'll be out in a bit. I need to be alone for a little longer."

Franki's hand stops gripping the doorframe, and her arm falls to her side. "OK. Let me know if you need anything. I'm here for you, Eli."

I nod. "Thank you, Franki. I can't say it enough." Franki stands in the doorway for another moment and then backs away slowly until she's gone.

When I return to the bar, I notice the conversations between people are louder and more energetic. I attribute that to the beer that everyone appears to enjoy. Gregory Bater, my father's childhood friend, is so drunk that his speech is slurred when he calls me over to tell me the same story he has told me twice already. I listen as he slaps me on the back. "He was proud of you, Eli. You know that, right? He was really proud of you." He keeps saying this over and over. I break from him, and that's when I see Ryah. She's wearing a formfitting black dress with a lace back. Her tan legs look thin and muscular as she stands in shiny black heels. She smiles at me before Franki approaches her to say hello. Ryah hugs Franki and then grips her hand as Franki speaks. Franki takes Ryah by the hand to introduce her to people. She looks at me again just before Susan and Tim say hello.

I haven't really listened to a word anyone has said for over two hours. People are drunk and laughing. I laugh too. I don't know why. I'm not happy. I'm not even sad. I feel numb. Bo arrives and shakes my hand. He offers a few kind remarks about my father. As he speaks to me, I notice his attention is directed elsewhere. When it's safe to check, I glance in the direction he's been looking and see Ryah talking to Franki at the bar. She looks back at us. Bo smiles at her. I leave Bo and grab a few empty plastic cups sitting on the bar and dispose of them in the trash can. Franki sees me doing this and walks over.

"Eli, what are you doing?" she asks in a concerned voice.

"Just cleaning up a bit. People are starting to leave, finally."

Franki places her hand on top of mine as I reach for another empty cup. "I'll clean this mess up later. Don't you worry about any of this."

"It's no big deal, Franki. I might as well make myself useful. I'm tired of talking to people."

Franki nods her head. "I understand. I'll clean this place up for you. You need to relax. Do you want to go home?"

I look over Franki's shoulder to see Ryah staring at us while smoking a cigarette. Her face is emotionless. I don't offer any response. Bo approaches her and says something. She looks at him with an annoyed expression. "I guess I am ready to leave," I say.

Franki squeezes my hand. "OK. I need to pack up the food and load the car with the cards and flowers."

"That's fine. No rush." As Franki gives me a hug, I see Bo say something to Ryah before turning from her and leaving.

I walk back to my office to wait on Franki. I know it will take her a while to finish everything because she is too kind to ignore anyone still at the bar. I sit at my desk with only a small lamp illuminating the otherwise dark room. I find myself staring into the darkness. I want to escape. The door to my office opens a crack. I hear the door creak as it opens farther and notice a figure standing in the doorway. I expect that it's Franki, but as my eyes focus, I notice it's not her.

"What are you doing?" I ask.

"I need to see you," she claims as she closes the door.

"Now?"

"Yes," she whispers as she locks the door behind her. She walks toward me. "Now."

"Ryah, Franki is taking me home," I say in a low voice.

"OK," she says. She stops beside my desk and looks down at me. "I don't care."

"She's your best friend."

"I want you."

I am immediately turned on. "I don't think…" Ryah leans down. She places her hand on my thigh. She runs her hand the full length of my thigh and back again. I can feel my heart beating. Her hand stops, and then she kisses me. I kiss her back as she grips me firmly in her hand. I pull her to me and tug her hair as we kiss passionately. Ryah unbuttons and unzips my pants as I raise her dress. She's not wearing any panties. I push my pants toward my knees frantically, and Ryah lowers herself on top of me. Ryah emits a muffled moan and then kisses me again.

***

A knock on the door comes just as Ryah is standing to fix her dress.

"Who is it?" I ask as I pull my pants up.

"Franki."

"Come on in," I say, knowing the door is locked.

"It's locked," she says as she tries to turn the knob. A panic seizes me. I look up at Ryah. She's smiling.

I stand just as Ryah removes her shoes and walks to the corner of the room without making a sound. I turn the lamp off and navigate my way to the door in the darkness. I take one more look at the corner of the room where Ryah stands before I unlock the door and open it. Before Franki can push her way inside, I block the entrance with my body and say, "I'm ready to leave."

"Were you sitting in the dark?"

"Yes. I needed a quiet place to think."

Franki doesn't question me as I exit the office and shut the door behind me. She reaches for my hand and holds it. She stops. For a second I fear what she may say. I smell like sex. *Can she smell it?* "Everything is going to be OK, Eli. I promise you. Everything will be OK."

CHAPTER THIRTY-ONE
Nobody is Perfect

Franki Rose

I sip hot tea from a mug as I look out my living room window. It's eleven in the morning on a Saturday in mid-September, and Eli still hasn't called. Last night he said he would call to tell me if he could accompany me to the sidewalk festival this weekend, but maybe he forgot. I don't know. Everything has been different since his dad died of a massive heart attack a week ago. I expected he might become distant, but it's as if he has shut down completely. He doesn't answer his phone, and when I visit him he is either away or asleep. He claims that he has to work more now, but I don't know if I believe him. I take another sip of tea. I stare at the tree outside my apartment and find a single yellow leaf. I watch it sway in the breeze. Fall has begun.

After I finish my tea, I decide to take a shower and get dressed. I still want to go to the sidewalk festival, and my mood isn't improving as I sit by myself waiting on a call from Eli that will likely never come. I put on some old button-fly jeans and a faded purple T-shirt with a frog on the front. I slide on my canvas shoes and check my hair in the mirror. It looks messy, but I don't care because Eli won't be there. I grab my ID and a twenty-dollar bill out of my billfold and shove the items in the front pocket of my jeans. I've always hated purses. I feel so awkward carrying them. I have no idea how Ryah makes it look sexy. Everything Ryah does is sexy. I'm never sexy. I'm only weird.

Downtown isn't crowded, but there are enough interesting people wandering from place to place that I'm glad I'm here. No one is in a hurry. I pass a couple, and they say hello. I don't know them, but I smile to be friendly. Before long, I'm saying hello to people I don't know. The friendliness is contagious. It's refreshing to see people taking time to enjoy the simple pleasures in life. I stop at a table where handmade friendship bracelets are for sale. There are two other people looking too. One is a teenage girl who looks familiar, but I can't place her. The other is a guy in his early twenties I don't know. I pick up a blue-and-white woven friendship bracelet. I inspect it casually, and when I place it back on the table I notice that the guy is looking at me. When I turn my head, he looks away. He has short brown hair and fair skin. He's wearing a red Coca Cola shirt and blue jeans with dark-brown boots. He is cute. I refocus my attention toward the bracelets on the table, but I want him to look at me again. I move to the other side of the table, and when I look up, he is gone. I feel disappointed. I lift an orange-and-red woven bracelet from the table, and that's when I hear someone say, "I like that one."

"Huh?" I utter. I cringe when I look up to see it's the cute guy.

"I said I like that bracelet." He smiles. I love his dimples.

"I'm sorry. You startled me." I can feel myself blushing.

He chuckles. I can't believe how adorable he is. I feel like a schoolgirl. "My apologies. I didn't mean to." His dark-brown eyes look directly at me. I look away.

"Don't worry about it. I'm glad someone recognizes my good taste."

"I'm John. What's your name?" He extends his hand to shake mine.

"Hi, John. I'm Franki." I shake his hand. Just his touch makes me short of breath.

"Nice to meet you, Franki. I love that name. Are you from here?"

"Born and raised, unfortunately. You?"

"Nope. I just moved here from Alaska."

"Alaska? That's fun. What made you move here?"

"Alaska is terrible. I lived in a small town where everyone knew each other. It was so boring."

I smile. "God help you."

He laughs. "Why do you say that?"

"That's how I would describe this town."

"I wouldn't say that. I've only been here a few weeks, but the people here seem pretty nice."

"At least the weather is nicer, I suppose."

"Exactly. I like your optimism. Plus, they don't have girls named Franki where I'm from." He smiles, and his dimples almost make me melt.

"You should flee while you can!"

John laughs. "What are you doing the rest of the day?" he asks.

"What do you mean?"

"Do you have any plans?"

"Not really. I'll probably check out a few other booths. Why?"

"Would you like to get a coffee or something?" The way he looks at me makes me feel special.

"I don't know."

"What's the problem?"

"Oh, no. There's no problem. I just...I don't know if I should."

"Well, Franki, you could make the safe decision here, and maybe we never see each other again. Or you could take a chance. Who knows, you might have some fun."

"I don't doubt that."

"Then what are we waiting for? Let's go."

I pause. I think about Eli as I look at John smiling back at me. I want to go so badly. "John, I want you to know that your offer is very tempting."

"But..."

"I'm sorry. I've been going through some tough times."

"Do you have a boyfriend?"

"Kinda. I don't know."

"Franki, if you were with me, you'd be able to answer that question without hesitation. But, hey, I understand. You seem like a great girl. I'd like to see you sometime if you ever change your mind."

"You never know. It was nice meeting you, John." I turn away from the table and take a step before John stops me.

"Wait."

"What?" I turn around to see him holding the orange-and-red bracelet.

"You forgot the bracelet."

"Oh. I don't think I'm going to buy it."

"Don't you like it?"

"I do, but—"

"Franki, forgive me for saying this, but you think too much. Let me buy it for you." "Oh, no. I couldn't let you do that."

"I insist." He moves past me to the woman working the booth. "Excuse me, I'd like to purchase this." John hands the woman twelve dollars and then turns and walks back to where I'm standing. I feel embarrassed.

"Thank you," I say while smiling.

"Don't mention it. Promise me one thing." He holds the bracelet out to me.

"What's that?" I ask.

"Promise me that this will not be the last time we see one another."

"John, you don't give up easily. OK. I promise."

"You promise what?"

I giggle. "I promise this will not be the last time we see one another."

"Perfect." He places the bracelet in my palm, and when I close my hand, I feel his thumb gently rub mine. I want the moment to last longer. I turn and walk away. Halfway down the street, I stop and look back.

John is still watching me. He offers a goofy wave that causes me to laugh. I wave back.

On my way home, I decide to stop by Eli's place. He still hasn't called. I worry about him. It must be horrible to find your deceased father sitting in his favorite chair wearing nothing but his boxers. Death has a way of stealing a person's dignity. Eli's car is parked in front of his father's house. I park my car behind his and walk to the front door and knock. I think I hear something, but Eli doesn't answer the door. I knock again. Still there is no response. *Where is he? What is he doing?* I look at my wrist at the bright orange-and-red bracelet and think about John waving good-bye.

CHAPTER THIRTY-TWO

Less is More

Kasey Price

My phone rings at two in the morning. I consider not answering, until I see who is calling. It's Ryah. When I say hello, all I can hear is crying and short breaths.

"What's the matter?" I ask, still trying to wake up.

"I can't…I can't…"

"I can barely understand what you're saying."

"I can't believe him," is all that she can utter.

"Where are you? Are you safe?"

"Yes." The sobbing continues between responses.

"Are you at your place?"

"I am now." I can hear her trying to compose herself.

I rub my eyes and sit up in bed. "Would you like to talk about it?"

"Can you come over?" she asks in a distraught voice.

"Ryah, it's two in the morning."

"Never mind," she says abruptly.

"Wait. Give me a second to wake up. Do you really want me to come over?"

There is a pause, but I can hear her breathing. "Yes. I want you to come over if you can. If you can't, I understand."

"Let me get dressed and I'll be over. You're not going to be asleep when I arrive, are you?"

"No."

"OK. Good."

"You don't have to come. I'll be all right."

"It's not a big deal, Ryah. I'm already getting dressed," I lie. "I'll be there in ten minutes."

"Thank you, Kasey. You're such a sweetheart."

I knock on Ryah's door twice before she answers. She opens the door slowly. The living room is completely dark. I step inside her apartment, and as my eyes acclimate to the darkness, I see Ryah is wearing a black tank top and short white cotton shorts. She looks stunning, even without trying. It looks as if she's wiping tears from her face, though I can't see if there are actually tears or if the gesture is done for effect.

"Hi," she says in a quiet voice.

I give her a hug, and she holds on to me tightly. "Are you OK?" I ask while still hugging her.

"I don't know," she replies. I loosen my grip. She clings to me a moment longer, which makes the inconvenience of visiting her at this hour worth it.

"What the hell happened?"

Ryah takes my hand and guides me down the hallway toward the only light on in the house, which happens to be in her bedroom. When we enter the room, she lets go of my hand and sits on the corner of the bed. I can see in the light that her eyes are red from crying, which causes me to feel guilty for thinking she may have concocted the whole scenario to gain attention.

"I don't know where to start. I feel lost," she says while staring at the floor. She keeps curling her toes against the carpet.

"If you don't feel comfortable..."

"It's Eli," she interrupts. "He's a fucking asshole."

"Eli Noor?"

"Yes."

"How do you know Eli? I thought you were seeing Bo?"

She avoids eye contact as she takes a deep breath. "I am. I mean I was. I don't know. Everything is so fucked up."

"What did Eli do?" I can feel my adrenaline surging. I don't know why, other than her admission was not expected.

"We've been...I don't know if I should tell you. Is this too strange for you?"

My surprise quickly transitions to seething anger. Ryah knows I still like her, yet she calls me over in the early morning to discuss her latest fling, and somehow she expects that I will be agreeable to this? *Is she really that fucking selfish?* I take a deep breath and say, "It's not strange."

"I've been seeing Eli," she admits.

"For how long?" I ask. A lump develops in my throat. I struggle to maintain my poise.

"Not that long, but long enough."

"What did he do?"

"It's more about what he doesn't do. I don't know where to begin." Ryah looks at me momentarily before looking back at the floor again.

"Why are you upset with him right now? Maybe that's where we should start."

"He told me he would call me. He always says he will call, but he never does. I don't know why I let him get to me so much. I shouldn't believe him. I shouldn't believe anyone. But it hurts. I guess I want to believe him. That's my problem."

"That's understandable," I say, despite the building rage I feel toward Ryah and Eli. "Did you try to call him?"

Ryah doesn't respond immediately. Her lip quivers as she fights the urge to cry. "I had to. I don't know why, but I had to call him."

"Don't get upset," I plead. No matter how much Ryah infuriates me, I still care. "Is his ignoring you the main issue then?"

"Yes and no. What hurts me the most is, I don't think he even cares."

"Then why are you with him?"

Ryah looks up at me as a single tear rolls down her left cheek and drips from her jaw onto the carpet. "I don't know."

While staring at Ryah, I realize that instead of being angry, I should calm myself and use this situation as an opportunity to improve my standing with her. I move over to the bed and sit next to her. She continues to look at the floor while curling her toes against the carpet. Her arms are folded and resting against her stomach.

"Come here," I say calmly. Ryah looks up as I move in to hug her. She puts her left arm around me as I bring her close. Her head rests against my shoulder as she submits to the embrace. I hug her tightly and wait for her to stop me. She doesn't.

"You deserve better," I eventually say as I continue to squeeze her body against mine. "Do you know that?"

"Thank you, Kasey." I can feel her take a deep breath. "I don't know what I'm going to do. I don't even know what I feel any longer."

"You need to do what is best for you," I say. I stop hugging her, and when she leans away from me, I look into her eyes. "You need to worry about you for a while."

"You're right. I don't know, though."

"What don't you know?"

"I don't know if I can stop feeling this way. I hate being sad. I hate the control Eli has over my emotions."

"Don't give him that control."

"You're right." Her eyes look past me as her mind wanders to a distant place. Without thinking, I lean toward Ryah and kiss her. She pulls away.

"What are you doing?" she asks in a panicked voice.

"I don't know. I'm sorry. It's just—"

"Kasey, we can't…I mean, I can't…"

"I know. It was stupid. I don't know what came over me. I'm sorry, Ryah." I remain next to her on the bed. Ryah stands up and walks to the doorway and stands with her back to me. "Ryah, I'm sorry. I just hate to see you this upset. I want you to see yourself how I see you."

Ryah turns around. Tears fall from both eyes. "Kasey, I think you better go."

"Ryah, don't do this. I'm sorry. It won't happen again. I care about you."

Ryah stands motionless. "You need to go," she repeats.

"Why?"

"Because I can't do this right now. I need a friend."

"I am your friend," I claim.

"That may be true, but right now I'm not strong enough to deal with the uncertainty."

"You don't trust me?"

Ryah looks directly at me. "I don't trust anyone."

CHAPTER THIRTY-THREE

Disingenuous

Bo Schnep

S he won't tell me what is wrong. Her silence disturbs me. I reach for her hand, but she doesn't return my grip. We walk past the playground and approach the picnic table that is shaded by the big oak tree. Two children scream and run in front of us on their way to the swings. I watch them chase each other and admire their innocence. Scarlett doesn't pay attention to them. She is distracted by whatever continues to haunt her. I don't know what to say, so I don't say anything. There's nothing more miserable than sharing a walk in the park on a sunny day with a sad girl.

Scarlett stares straight ahead as we sit at the picnic table. When I turn my head to see what she's looking at, I realize that she's not really looking at anything in particular. I feel my phone vibrate in my pocket, but I don't check it. Something is wrong with Scarlett, and I'm not sure what it is.

"Have you noticed the change?" she asks before blinking and turning her head to look at me.

"What change?" I say, confused.

"The leaves have started to change color. Haven't you noticed?"

I think about it for a moment. "I guess I haven't paid much attention."

Scarlett looks back toward the children, who are swinging and gig-gling. "The days are getting shorter and the nights are getting colder. Summer is almost over for another year."

I don't know how to respond to Scarlett. My silence doesn't appear to upset her at all. I question if she's even talking to me. I suspect maybe she's talking to herself.

"See?" Scarlett reaches down and plucks a leaf from the ground. The leaf is green with gold edges. "The transformation is happening. It's gradual at first, and then it's over and the trees are bare."

"Are you OK?" I ask, not knowing what else to say. Her riddles aren't making any sense to me.

"I'm fine," she says in a monotone voice. She pinches the leaf's stem between her forefinger and thumb and twirls it. "Do you care about me?" she asks.

"What? Of course I care about you," I blurt, without thinking.

Scarlett's attention remains directed toward the leaf she twirls. She appears utterly indifferent to my reply. "Are you sure?"

"Yes, I'm sure. Why would you ask me that question?" I look at Scarlett. She loosens her grip gradually and allows the leaf to fall from her hand. It lands on the ground in front of her. One of the children on the swing screams. I look at them and then look back at Scarlett. Her eyes look glassy, and then a tear escapes and rolls down her cheek. "Scarlett, what's wrong? Why are you crying?"

"I don't know," she says in a flat tone.

"There has to be a reason."

"I don't think you care about me. I guess that may be why I'm sad. Maybe that's not the reason. I don't know."

"Why don't you think I care about you?" There's a long pause. Scarlett takes a deep breath and wipes the tear from her cheek.

"I don't think I can live a lie, Bo. It makes me too sad." My mouth feels dry. *Does Scarlett know?*

"I'm not asking you to live a lie," I say. I clear my throat after I notice my voice sounds shaky.

"OK."

"You don't believe me, do you?"

"I guess I have to believe you."

"Don't make it sound so forced."

My phone vibrates in my pocket again. I sigh audibly and hope Scarlett will abandon her preoccupation with interrogating me. I take my phone from my pocket. There are four unread text messages from Ryah. I open them to reveal a lengthy text that was divided into multiple messages. They say, "I'm sorry. Bo, I'm sorry. Can you forgive me? I don't know what's wrong with me. I always ruin what is good. I don't know why I'm so self-destructive. Will you forgive me? Why aren't you answering? Will you see me? You can cuss me out and yell at me if that will make you feel better, just don't ignore me. Please see me." I close the messages and feel torn. I really want to visit Ryah, but after the way she treated me at Wayside, I'm beginning to think that she has been using me all along. Scarlett isn't anything like Ryah. She is trustworthy. She wants me to care for her. Ryah only wants me when it's convenient for her. Scarlett is staring at the ground. I put my hand on her knee and squeeze her leg. She moves her hand and rubs my arm. A gust of wind lifts the green leaf with gold edges from the grass. I watch as the wind carries it away. The children yell as they run past us. Maybe change isn't so bad.

CHAPTER THIRTY-FOUR

Wounded by Pleasure

Ryah Klein

I remember when I was a little girl and Francis Duffy gave me my first love note. It said something cute about him liking me and how I was prettier than the prettiest flower. I don't know why, but I showed all of my friends that note at recess, and everyone made fun of Francis for the next two years. The boys called him Flower Francis and Francis the Fairy. I'm not sure why I did that. Maybe I perceived his kindness as weakness. Francis moved away in the seventh grade. I always wondered what happened to him.

Ever since I can remember, I've been driven by pleasure. I like attention and how it makes me feel. I don't apologize for it because I'm not sorry. I smoked my first cigarette in fourth grade after school at Nicole's house before her mother came home. I coughed a lot, but I remember the way her big brother looked at me. I kissed my first boy when I was in sixth grade, on top of the slide at recess. All of my friends couldn't believe I actually did it. When I came down the slide after William, I remember how the other girls huddled around me on the playground and asked me for details. Two days later I told William's friends to tell him not to talk to me anymore. The first kiss that mattered came years later, but it lacked something. The meaning I attached to that later kiss detracted from the pleasure in some way. There's something visceral about pleasing oneself. There's an honesty in selfishness.

I open the door for Bo, and he walks inside my apartment. I haven't seen him since the night at Wayside when we argued. I don't know what we argued about, so I'm assuming it was feigned so I could find Eli. Eli never changes, though. He's not calling me or visiting me now. Maybe nobody ever really changes. Maybe people just act like they do. I don't know. I look at Bo. He is trying his best to look angry, but I can tell that he forgave me as soon as he stepped inside my apartment.

"Ryah, I can't stay long. What did you want to see me about?"

I shut the door and look at Bo. He's wearing a pressed white button-down shirt with a black-and-silver patterned tie hanging loosely around his neck. His black pants look new. His hair is longer, and it makes him look younger.

"Relax, Bo. Do you want something to drink?" I ask in a soft voice.

"Don't do that, Ryah," he warns.

"Do what?"

"Don't act like everything is OK." His hostility only gives me more confidence.

"Everything is OK, isn't it? I mean, why wouldn't everything be OK?"

"Did you really want me to visit you so you could speak in circles? If so, I'll see myself out."

"No…"

"I'm serious, Ryah. I have better things to do. Not everyone enjoys your goddamn games. In fact, I think you're the only one who enjoys them."

"I'm not playing games, Bo."

"Well then, what is it? Why did you want to see me?"

I clear my throat. "I want to apologize for our argument. I think I was drunk, but that's no excuse for being a bitch to you. You don't deserve that. I'm sorry…" I allow my voice to trail off at the end. I can tell Bo is listening, because he doesn't respond immediately. He only looks at me in an attempt to determine if I'm being sincere.

"Ryah, I can't believe you're actually admitting fault." Bo's expression relaxes. He appears as though me wants to comfort me.

"I don't know what's wrong with me," I continue. "I have a tendency to damage everyone close to me."

Bo moves closer to me and squeezes my right forearm with his left hand. "Nothing is wrong with you, Ryah."

I look at the floor. "Something is wrong with me, Bo. Why else would I act the way I do? I don't know who I am."

"Ryah, there's no need to be so hard on yourself. You're a great girl. I don't know if I could ever get over you fully." I look up from the floor and stare at Bo. "But I can't continue this cycle of you liking me one minute and hating me the next. It's not fair to me. Maybe you should take some time for yourself and figure out what you want."

"What are you saying?" I ask, still looking directly at Bo. His hand lets go of my arm.

"I'm saying that I'm seeing someone else."

"What? Are you serious?" The admission turns my stomach. *How long has he been seeing the other woman?*

"I thought you should hear it from me in person. I'm not telling you this to hurt you. We both tried to make this work. It's not anyone's fault."

I feel like crying. I can't tell if it's because I'm angry or sad. "Get out, Bo," I command.

"Ryah, there's no reason to be angry."

"Don't tell me how to feel."

"You're being unreasonable."

"I'm being unreasonable?" I take a step toward Bo. "I'm the one being unreasonable? We get in an argument and you immediately start seeing someone else? Is that reasonable?"

Bo looks calm. "You don't want to be with me, Ryah."

"What do you mean, I don't want to be with you?"

"Exactly what I said. You don't want to be with me. If you did, none of this would be happening."

"Get out!" I repeat.

"Why are you pushing me out, Ryah? Is it because you didn't get your way? Is it because for the first time in your privileged life someone actually didn't bend to your will? Is it because deep down you know I'm right?

"Bo, get the hell out of my apartment and don't come back." I shove him toward the door.

"I don't know why you're acting this way. You're just going to call one of your other guys."

"Get the fuck out!"

Bo turns and walks toward the door. I follow closely behind him. Bo opens the door and goes to close it behind him, but I catch it before it latches shut and force it open.

"Don't call me or text me ever again. It's over!" I yell as he gets into his car and speeds away. I slam the door shut and press my back against it. Suddenly tears stream from my eyes. I crouch down so that my knees are in my chest. I hold myself and cry.

CHAPTER THIRTY-FIVE
Anniversary

Scarlett Davison

I look at his number displayed on my phone's screen and want to call him, but I don't. It's the twenty-fourth of September, and I wonder if he is thinking about that morning two years ago when I left the house. I said I was going to see a friend, but I didn't. Instead I went to the clinic. I still have dreams in which I am preparing to leave for the clinic that day. In the dream, I try to stop myself, but I can't. He knew when I returned home that something had changed. I didn't have to tell him. He knew it when he looked into my eyes. When I saw the sadness on his face, I lost it. I thought our love was strong enough to endure the abortion. I thought I was doing the right thing for us. I thought...

I walk into the kitchen and pour a glass of cheap white wine. I look at the wine in the glass. I leave the glass of wine on the counter without taking a drink and walk out of the kitchen. I can see the sidewalk from my living room window. Sometimes I watch people walk by my house and ponder where they are going. I haven't done that in a while. Ms. Malone's dog is barking again. The sun is setting in the sky. Dark orange and violet streaks color the horizon. I feel a moment of utter peace, and before it can escape me, I press the call button. His phone rings.

***

When I hear his car pull into the driveway, I immediately get up from the chair and check myself in the mirror. I should have changed my shirt. I'm wearing a red tank top with my old blue jeans. I consider running to my bedroom but abandon that thought when I hear him knock on the front door. I freeze. I used to live with him, and now I can't even bring myself to answer the door. A second knock sounds. I take slow steps toward the door. I open it and see him. It's been so long. He looks so good.

His dark hair stretches past the collar of his yellow button-down shirt. His jeans look new. I look at him from the doorway. I crave him so badly. For a moment his mask of uncaring vanishes and I can tell he has missed me. I think he missed me. *I hope he missed me.*

"Come in," I finally muster in a shaky voice. He doesn't say anything. He enters my home and looks around, but he doesn't appear to be overly curious. Instead he appears to be indifferent. *Can he tell that I am terrified?* I close the door and walk to my living room. He follows me. I turn around and he stops. I look at him and then hug him without warning. He hugs me back, almost reflexively.

"I've missed you," I say as I'm squeezing him.

"I missed you too," he admits.

I let go of him and motion for him to sit on the couch. He does, but he sits on the edge of the cushion in a guarded way. I lean back. I feel like I might cry. I tell myself that I can't.

"I'm sorry about your dad," I say finally. "I thought about you that whole day."

"I appreciate that. It has been difficult."

"Eli, I hope you know I never stopped caring about you."

He looks at me with such a fixed gaze that I feel unsettled. "I know," he says. His stare becomes distant.

"I wanted so badly to be there for you. I know that's not what you want to hear, but it's how I felt. I'm sorry."

Eli doesn't say anything. He looks at the floor. I want to hold his hand just to feel his skin against mine. I look at him and a deep sense of desperation overwhelms me.

"How have you been?" he asks.

"I've been OK."

"That's good." He looks around the room to avoid eye contact. It saddens me that we've become reduced to such trivial exchanges when at one time we had planned to spend our lives together. Time changes everything.

"Do you ever think about…?" I don't finish my sentence and instead look away.

"Think about what?" Eli looks at me.

"Never mind." Silence follows, and Eli becomes noticeably uncomfortable.

"Scarlett, I think I better go," Eli says in a flat tone.

"You don't have to."

"I know. You've been very kind to me, and I appreciate it. It helps to see you."

"It helps me too."

Eli stands and walks toward the door. I stand and move toward him. I want him to stay, but I don't want to reveal my weakness. Eli turns to face me. He offers a faint smile. I can't tell if it's forced. I hug him. He hugs me back.

"I'm sorry," I mutter while still squeezing Eli. I feel his arms loosen around me. "I'm sorry for everything, Eli."

"Let's not do this to ourselves," he pleads. "It won't change anything."

"Do you ever think about the way things were between us?" I ask. "I mean, do you ever remember the good times we shared? We had something special once."

Eli lets go of me and looks into my eyes. "It doesn't do any good to think of the past." He stands in front of me, waiting on my reaction. I can't breathe. I feel lightheaded. My vision loses focus. Eli's stare remains fixed. Then he opens the door and leaves.

CHAPTER THIRTY-SIX
Naïve Honesty

Kasey Price

I feel alone. I feel underappreciated. I suddenly regret my mistakes. I loathe myself for being so gullible. I detest trust. I want to make sure that Franki doesn't succumb to the same cynicism. It's the least that I can do.

Franki is already seated on the bench near the birch tree when I arrive. The bench used to be our favorite place in the entire town because it is situated on a hill and overlooks the river. I stop for a moment and look at her. Her brown hair is tousled from the wind. It's cool enough that she's wearing jeans and her favorite canvas shoes. The bulky hooded jacket she's wearing is unzipped. She looks so beautiful sitting in the shade as the sun reflects off the moving water. I sometimes wonder why I couldn't love her more. Maybe she's too pure.

When Franki sees me approaching, she smiles. Her genuineness uplifts my mood. She may be the last person who truly cares.

"How are you, Kasey?" she asks as I sit beside her on the bench. The river looks high. I watch the water moving. Birds sing in the distance. I can't remember the last time I took the opportunity to listen.

"I'm OK. How are you?" I turn my head to look at her. She's squinting and using her hand to shield her eyes from the sun. I notice a bright orange-and-red bracelet on her wrist. I think of Eli and cringe.

"I'm doing…well, I'm doing," she says, followed by a halfhearted laugh. "Why did you want to see me?"

"It's always nice to see you. You may be the only trustworthy person I know," I say, and I mean it.

"Thank you, Kasey. Lately I've been feeling like that's not necessarily benefiting me." As I look at Franki, I think of all the times I was with her and took her for granted.

"I don't know of an easy way to say this," I begin.

"Say what?"

I pause and look down. Sweat forms on my forehead. A gust of wind provides relief.

"What is it, Kasey?"

I look up at her. "Are you still seeing Eli?"

"Yes…well, kinda. I don't know. He's been so difficult to read since his father passed. Why do you ask? Do you know Eli?"

I detect Franki's confusion. I consider abandoning my whole agenda but then decide she must know. "I don't know Eli. I only know who he is."

"Oh," she murmurs.

"I think he's seeing Ryah," I blurt. "In fact, I am certain of it."

Franki doesn't immediately respond. She doesn't blink. Her face is frozen in disbelief.

"I'm sorry I am the one who is telling you this." I watch her for a moment.

Franki blinks. "Ryah Klein?"

"Yes."

"The Ryah Klein who is my best friend?"

"Yes."

"Who told you this?" she asks before she looks away from me. She stares at the river. I can't tell what she's feeling.

"I'd rather not say, but it's reliable."

Franki doesn't move. Her breaths are shallow.

"Don't hate me."

There is a long period of silence. I turn from her and face the river as well. No detectable emotion is present on her face. Even her posture remains rigid.

"Franki, will you please say something?" I beg.

Franki turns her head slowly to face me. "What is there to say?" she utters.

I suddenly regret telling her. "Do you want me to leave?" I ask, not knowing what to do. She doesn't respond. "Franki?"

"Do I want you to leave?" she repeats my question. "I don't care. Nothing matters, does it?"

I don't say anything. Instead, I sit next to her and look out at the rippling water as the birds chirp and the wind causes the tree branches to sway.

CHAPTER THIRTY-SEVEN

Listlessness

Elijah Noor

I sometimes dream of a bleeding star that gradually fades into the blackness of the night. As I drive to meet Franki, I think of this. She must know something. The pained tone of her voice on the phone caused me to regret returning her call. I'm not sure what she knows. Even if I did know, I don't think that it would matter. I can't afford to confess my sins to her. If even the slightest element of doubt exists, Franki will hope that what is, isn't. That's human nature. Truth has no consequence on a person's daily life. What is believed to be true is all that matters.

When I arrive, I find her sitting on the steps of her porch. Her eyes are red. I surmise she's been crying, though I don't ask. I walk up to her and stand directly in front of her. She looks at me and offers a feigned smile. I find her distress uncomfortable. I shouldn't have visited.

"How are you?" I ask as I sit next to her on the steps. Franki doesn't move, though her body language indicates vulnerability.

"I've been better," she says in a low, sad voice. I stare ahead at the road. A blue four-door car passes. A man in a neighboring yard looks at us as he smokes a cigarette before he busies himself with moving bulging plastic bags from his garage to the curb. I look up at the blue sky. I want more than anything to see a bird flying overhead. I don't see one.

"What's wrong, Franki?" I ask, feeling the silence becoming unbearable.

She turns her head. Franki purses her lips. Her restraint is visible. She sighs. A look of pervasive sorrow follows. "You don't know?" she asks finally.

"Should I?" I remain aloof. Franki doesn't persist with questions. Her defeated demeanor depresses me.

"I know about Ryah." She looks at me after speaking and then looks down at her hands. I don't say anything. "Is it true?" There is a pause. I don't speak. "Never mind. I guess I have been foolish. I'm embarrassed."

"I don't know what to say."

"You don't have to say anything. This is my fault, in a way. Though, I have to know, do you want to be with her?" Her desperation is palpable.

"Be with her? What kind of question is that?" I ask, indignant.

"Just answer my question, Eli."

"How did you get such an idea? Who's been lying to you?"

"That's something I would love to know." Franki turns her head and stares straight ahead at the street.

"Are we not going to actually talk about this?"

"What? That's what I'm trying to do. I'm trying to talk to you about this."

"No, you're not. You're assuming that an idiotic rumor is true when it's not. I refuse to entertain rumors."

She turns to face me. "Kasey told me, OK? Kasey said you've been seeing Ryah behind my back."

"Kasey Price?" I ask, knowing the answer.

"Yes." Franki sounds as if she may cry at any moment. I hope she doesn't.

I nod my head. "That makes sense then," I say with conviction.

Franki's disposition changes from confident to unsure. "What do you mean?"

"Franki, didn't you consider why Kasey Price would say such a thing to you?"

"I'm not following you. What should I consider?"

"You're so caring that you immediately believe others are equally as caring. Kasey wants you back, and this is his ploy to accomplish his goal," I state confidently.

"That's not true, Eli. Kasey knows it's over between us."

"You've been torturing yourself over this, haven't you? Damn, Franki. I know Kasey has talked to you about his feelings for you."

"No, he hasn't," she retorts defiantly.

"You may not have interpreted it that way, but if you stop and think about it, you can probably pinpoint a moment when he said something that revealed that he wasn't over you." Franki is silent. "It's simple to me. In fact, it's a bold move. Kasey must really know how to persuade you." Franki's brow furrows.

"Maybe you're right," she says after an extended silence. "I guess I hadn't considered that possibility."

"I'm sorry you've been so distraught," I say while smiling at her.

"I guess I shouldn't trust people so readily."

I look out at the street and watch a few cars drive by. A police siren sounds somewhere in town.

"How are you so good at understanding people's motivations?"

I look up at the sky as if I'm deep in thought. I see the shape of the clouds change ever so slowly. I then say, "Only after a person has their heart broken does the world appear as it truly is."

Franki appears dissatisfied with my answer. "And how is that?"

CHAPTER THIRTY-EIGHT
Kiss and Make Up

Ryah Klein

I find myself downtown, sitting on a bench near the train station, watching people and listening to bits and pieces of their conversations. A young boy and girl argue over a penny they found nearby. The girl throws it across the railroad tracks and then laughs in a mocking way. The little boy cries and runs to his mother, who scolds both of them. She tells them to grow up. I want to stop her and tell her that growing up is the last thing she should be telling kids to do. A couple looks on from the bench opposite mine and smiles dumbly. I stare at them with disdain. Maybe the absence of love has dulled my sensibilities. A young man strides by without looking at anyone. *How can I feel so alone when I'm surrounded by people?*

I send out the same text to five different guys. It says, "I hope you're well." It amazes me how even the most impersonal messages are immediately personalized by those who receive them. I stand up and move closer to the tracks. I think of the time when I was a child and placed ten pennies on the tracks so they would be smashed by the train. I recovered all but one and kept them in my desk drawer for years. I would sometimes take them out of the drawer and admire the distorted faces on the coins. Those were confusing times, when other kids my age were probably praying to God or something. I don't think I ever believed that prayers come true.

***

I'm sitting in a small restaurant near a window facing Main Street. My hot tea is delivered by a girl who smiles too much. I sip the mint tea and watch people passing by the window. Some of them look at me as they walk by. Three of the guys I texted reply. I have lost interest, though, and don't respond, even though Greg keeps sending me text messages. While looking out at the street, I catch a glimpse of my reflection in the window. My hair looks better than I remember it looking when I left my apartment. When my eyes refocus, I see a man smiling at me. Apparently he thinks I was looking at him. I grimace and turn away. My phone vibrates with an incoming text.

Eli's text message says, "I've been better. What are you doing? Can I see you?" Suddenly I'm overcome with excitement that quickly transitions into anxiety. I didn't think he would respond. I take a drink of the now-warm tea. I feel sick. I look up at the neighboring table as the smiling server relays the lunch specials. Her happiness annoys me. I may not leave her a tip. I look down at my phone again. *What should I do?*

I arrive at Eli's new address. His father's house is the largest one on the block. I realize as I knock on the front door that there is so much about Eli I don't know. He opens the door. I look up at him as a lump forms in my throat.

"Come in," he says. As I walk past, he comments, "Please excuse the boxes. I don't have the energy to unpack them." I stand in the entranceway as he closes the door. I look around the house and admire the vastness. It has nice dark-colored hardwood floors and a vaulted ceiling in the living room. The furniture is old and expensive. Boxes and clothes on hangers clutter the otherwise immaculate room. An antique grandfather clock chimes.

I regain my confidence when I sit next to Eli on the couch. I feel most comfortable when I'm close to him. He looks sad.

"What's wrong, Eli?" I ask. I want to kiss his lips. I crave his touch so badly.

"I moved here last weekend and I can't get used to it."

I don't know what to say. I've never been in a position where I wanted to comfort someone.

He looks away and continues, "Ever since my father died, I have been fixated on death. The priest talked on and on at the funeral about the afterlife and how my father was resting now and how one day we would be reunited. I don't believe a word he said. We won't be reunited. He's dead. I don't think there's anything after we die. When life is over, we are over. It's that simple."

I panic when I try to remember what it's like to join my body with Eli's and instead remember other men. "I agree with you," I say. I place my hand on Eli's.

***

I lay my head on Eli's bare chest as we lie in his bed. His beating heart sounds against my ear. I look up at him and see that he is looking at the ceiling. I don't ask what he's thinking about. I close my eyes and savor his scent. I consider what Eli said to me about his father. *One day I will be dead.* I squeeze Eli. His hand rubs my back. My legs still tremble from the pleasure. I am right where I belong.

CHAPTER THIRTY-NINE
Someone Knows

Bo Schnep

I once met a girl at church camp who believed that life has no meaning. I didn't say anything to her, but I remember that I couldn't sleep that night. I felt so empty. Years later I feel that same empty feeling. I guess it has something to do with my understanding that maybe that girl was right. I look at my watch. It's almost six o'clock. Franki will be finished with work soon.

Franki doesn't notice my car as she exits the café. I get out of my car and approach her. She looks tired. Strands of brown hair that have escaped from her ponytail hang over her face. She is so distracted by her phone that I feel it necessary to announce my presence so I don't startle her.

"Franki," I say in a soft tone. She looks up and smiles once she realizes it's me.

"Bo. How are you?" she asks in the most cheerful tone she can muster.

"I'm OK. How are you?"

Her smile fades. "I'm worn out. It's been a long day."

"Listen," I interject, "Can I speak to you about Ryah?" Franki's expression quickly changes to concern.

"Is she OK?" she asks.

"Oh, Ryah's fine. It's nothing too serious."

"OK. Good. Well, I was about to go home and start dinner. Would you want to come over?"

"I don't mean to inconvenience you."

"Oh, no. It's no trouble, really."

I follow Franki's car to her house. She retrieves her mail and then leads me inside her apartment. I can see her living room and kitchen from the entranceway. A wind chime made of metal forks and spoons hangs over her kitchen sink. A mannequin torso sits in the corner of her living room. Franki throws her mail and her keys on a cheap TV tray table that is stationed along the wall of the entranceway. I watch as she continues to her kitchen.

"Do you want anything to drink?" she yells to me. "I have a few light beers."

"Sure." I pick up a black umbrella with visible holes in the canopy. I don't bother to ask why she has it. Everything in Franki's apartment appears to have no real function, but it somehow fits. I don't understand any of it.

"Come on in. You don't have to stand by the door," Franki imparts while handing me the cold bottle of beer. She leads me to the living room and sits cross-legged in a wooden rocking chair. She takes a drink from her beer and sets the bottle on the floor beside her. She rocks a few times. I sit down in a chair decorated with a pattern of bright-yellow flowers. "So what would you like to talk about?"

I take a drink. "Have you noticed anything different about Ryah?" I ask.

Franki taps her chin with her index finger. "Different in what way? Ryah has always been different."

"I mean, she seems more distant lately. I'm worried because she won't talk to me, and I figured that maybe she had talked to you. You don't have to reveal anything to me. I only want to make sure she's OK."

I look at Franki after I speak. Her reaction reveals nothing. I can't tell if she knows anything or not.

"Bo, I haven't talked to her very much recently. I don't want to go into everything, but I heard a rumor that upset me, and I haven't been talking to many of my friends."

"I'm sorry to hear that. Are you all right?" I continue to study Franki. She may be the most authentic person in this town. She also may be the most helpless.

"I'll be fine. Thankfully it was only a rumor. You know how that goes in a small town. God, if there weren't any rumors to distract people, everyone might have to actually focus on improving their own lives." Franki chuckles after she says this.

I suddenly have the urge to leave. I'm overcome with sadness. Franki's optimism is apparent. She rocks back and forth in the chair, waiting for me to speak. Her trust in others is her greatest mistake. Maybe I have believed in the wrong people all along.

CHAPTER FORTY
Hope

Franki Rose

When I was a little girl, my grandmother told me that the greatest gift bestowed upon humanity was hope. As I sat on her lap and smelled her strong perfume, I remember not knowing what she meant. I didn't ask her, though, and she didn't clarify. My grandmother became very ill two weeks later. She was later admitted to the hospital, where a doctor diagnosed her with brain cancer. She passed on a Friday, exactly four months after being diagnosed with the disease. I was in the hospital room with her when she died. I heard the beeping machines and watched her chest rise and fall as she struggled for breath. Then she stopped breathing and it was over.

I look at Eli from the passenger seat as he drives. I try to forget all of those painful memories. We are headed to Ludlow Falls to enjoy the waterfall. Eli thinks a weekend trip is what we need. I agree. I admire the way the sunlight shines on his face. He is so handsome. I don't know how I ever thought he could harm me. Eli looks over at me and smiles. It's so nice to have him all to myself.

Eli parks the car and removes the blanket from the trunk for us to sit on. I follow him as we walk toward the bridge. I can hear the rushing water before I can see it. Eli lays the blanket on the ground just beneath the bridge. I admire the white foam produced by the falling water. It's so beautiful. I look over to find that Eli isn't sitting next to me any longer. I swing my head around and find him standing by the concrete base supporting the bridge. He motions for me to join him. *What is he up to?*

I walk over to Eli and hug him. He hugs me back with one arm. He's smiling.

"What?" I ask, not sure what he's thinking.

"Look what I have." He pulls a black marker from his pocket.

"What are you going to do with that?"

His grin gets bigger. "I thought we should commemorate this occasion."

"You're not going to—"

"What?"

"We can't write graffiti." Eli uncaps the marker. "Seriously…" He pushes the tip against the concrete. "Eli!"

"It's too late. We have to finish it now." I give Eli a look of disapproval, but really I think it's sweet. He writes *Eli + Franki*. "We're the only ones who will know what this means. It's small enough it won't be noticeable to anyone who isn't looking for it." It's the sweetest thing Eli has ever done for me.

Eli and I return to the blanket and hold hands while watching the water flowing past us. I don't think I've ever seen Eli look more peaceful. His smile looks different than it does most of the time. I lay my head on his shoulder.

"I'm glad you brought me here," I say to him in a low voice, barely audible over the sound of the rushing water.

"I am too. I wish life could always be like this." I squeeze Eli's arm. The water keeps coming. The water keeps crashing.

CHAPTER FORTY-ONE
Choices

Elijah Noor

Detachment is a disease that festers until uncaring is no longer a choice. I'm on my way to visit Scarlett after returning from my trip with Franki. I should feel guilty. I know I should, but I had to get out of town for the weekend. Ryah won't stop texting me. She's been frantic recently. I don't think she can accept the way things are between us any longer. She wants what she can't have. I guess everyone does.

Scarlett answers the door. Her presence used to instill in me a belief in love, but now when I see her standing in the doorway smiling, I think only of what has happened in the past and what will likely happen in the future. She's wearing a plaid flannel-style button-up with the top two buttons undone. The dark jeans she is wearing complement her figure nicely. I walk inside her home and feel so uncomfortable that I want to leave, but I can't. I have to see her. She closes the door.

"I have to admit, I was a bit shocked when I got your message that you wanted to see me. Don't get me wrong, I am overjoyed, but shocked," Scarlett says as she moves closer and hugs me.

I feel the flesh of her arms touch the back of my neck. Her body presses against mine. My mind is blank.

"Please, have a seat."

I sit on the couch next to Scarlett. Her excitement is apparent. She twirls her hair with her index finger the same way she used to. She hasn't changed. I have.

"What's wrong, Eli? I can tell something is bothering you," she says in a caring voice. I can feel myself recoil a bit.

"I don't know exactly," I say as I attempt to conceal my contempt.

"You can tell me. It's me, remember?"

I lean forward as if I'm going to say something, and then I don't.

"Do you want something to drink?"

"Yes. Please."

Scarlett gets up and walks to the kitchen. I watch her leave the room.

Scarlett returns to the living room and hands me a glass of water. I take a drink as she resumes her seat beside me. I experience déjà vu. I take another drink of water.

"Eli—" Scarlett begins.

"The last time I felt anything was when I was with you. When we broke up…" I pause purposefully. Scarlett's body language suggests concern. "Do you think that life can injure some people permanently?"

Scarlett's expression transitions to one of contemplation. She takes a deep breath. "I hope not," she replies. "I mean, I guess it's possible, but I think that hopelessness is a choice. Why, is that how you feel?" The question stings me in an unexpected way. I look away from her and take a drink. "Do you feel that way, Eli?" she presses.

"I don't know. It's been difficult since everything happened between us." I look back to Scarlett. Her eyes are no longer focused on me. She looks sad. I wonder if the pain of the past haunts her often.

"Eli, do you remember when we bought that puppy, and before we could name her, she was hit by a car?"

I resent Scarlett's question. "Of course I remember that. Why would you bring it up?"

"Because that's the only time I ever saw you cry. I wanted to comfort you so badly, but you wouldn't let me near you until you finished burying her in the backyard. That night I put my arms around you and told you to always remember my embrace when you felt hurt or sad. It's an uncaring world. All we can do is comfort one another and persevere."

Somewhere a fly buzzes against the inside of a window. "This world is uncaring," I confirm in a flat voice.

"Come here," Scarlett urges. I look at her, and when I don't move, she moves over to me. She wraps her arms around me and hugs me. "I never stopped loving you, Eli," she says. She rubs the middle of my back with one hand while the other one strokes my hair. I smile as I consider how well the visit is going. "Eli, I want you to stay with me tonight." I can still feel her fingers kneading my back. "Will you stay with me?"

CHAPTER FORTY-TWO
Unexpected Proposal

Scarlett Davison

"I know things haven't been going so well between us," Bo begins. We're sitting along the edge of the pond at his parents' place. He said that he had something important to discuss with me. We haven't really talked to each other much in the past few weeks. I suspect that this is his way of ending our relationship. I don't disagree with his decision. Breakups are never easy.

"I want to accept responsibility for the rift that has developed," Bo continues. "It's my fault. I have been selfish and preoccupied with other things. I know that now." I look at Bo and prepare to reveal my disappointment when he tells me it's over. I am impressed that he has gone to the effort he has to ensure that I will be protected as much as possible. It shows a maturity I didn't know he possessed. "I also know that I have taken you for granted." Here it comes. I ready myself for the moment. Bo stops talking.

"It's OK, Bo. I think I understand what you are trying to say." I reach for his hand and squeeze it in mine.

"You do?" he asks. His face contorts with confusion.

"I respect your honesty. We have shared so many wonderful memories together," I affirm.

"I agree. That's what has caused me to consider what my life would be like without you," he admits. Bo lets go of my hand. I nod my head and look down. I pluck a blade of grass and admire it. It feels smooth. "Scarlett, the reason I brought you here is to…" Bo pauses again. When I look up, I see him positioned on one knee. "Scarlett, will you marry me?" he asks.

Once I catch my breath, I say, "Bo," just as he produces a diamond ring from his pocket.

He looks at me with expectant eyes.

"I thought…"

"I've thought about this too," Bo concedes. "I know our relationship hasn't been perfect, but I want us to work. You make me a better person, Scarlett. I didn't understand that until recently."

I look at the ring and then back to Bo. His blond curls make him look so endearing. "I don't know what to say. I'm speechless."

"Say yes. If you say yes, I promise you I won't disappoint you again. We can build a life together."

"I…Bo, it's…you're…" I can't finish a single thought.

"There's no rush," Bo says after witnessing my floundering. "I love you, and that's not going to change." He slides the ring back into his pocket.

"I'm not saying no," I impart after I regain my poise. "It's just so unexpected."

"There's no need to explain. The ring isn't going anywhere, and neither am I," Bo promises while patting the pocket he placed the ring in with his hand.

"Are you sure it's all right if I think about it?"

"Absolutely," he says cheerfully. Bo looks more relaxed. I look at the tall grass surrounding the edge of the pond and see a multicolored dragonfly resting on a tall thistly weed.

CHAPTER FORTY-THREE
Uncertainty

Bo Schnep

T he only reprieve from the mindless tedium that accompanies investigating graffiti painted on the Main Street Bridge the night before or solving the mystery of who stole Mr. Culver's lawn ornaments comes in the form of a car accident or the infrequent suicide. Needless to say, my life lacks substance. I have only come to understand that recently. The monotony gets to me. Days blur into nights, and nights blur into days. After seeing people disfigured beyond recognition when their car inexplicably hits a telephone pole or after studying a bloated body of a deceased person who hasn't been discovered for a week, it's hard to believe that there's any meaning to life. I guess I need something to look forward to. Maybe that would help in some way.

After my shift I stop by Wayside for a drink. Eli is working the bar, but he doesn't say much more than an obligatory hello. I sit at the far end of the bar, take my phone from my pocket, and place it on the bar in front of me. I loosen my tie before taking a drink of beer. I take a deep breath and attempt to forget my entire day. I take another drink. I set the bottle on the bar and pick up my phone. I send a text to Scarlett. She doesn't respond. It's possible that she's in bed already. I take another drink of beer and try to distract myself by watching the television, but it's already after nine o'clock, and all that's on are some sports highlights that don't interest me. I pick up my phone again and text Ryah that I hope she's well. I haven't talked to her since I proposed to Scarlett. I want to be a different person.

I order a second drink, and Eli provides it without saying a word. I watch him as he walks away. He stands at the other side of the bar and busies himself. There are only a handful of patrons present, and I can't help but question why Eli is being so distant. My phone vibrates on the bar, and I pick it up. It's a text from Ryah. Her reply says, "I've been better." She doesn't offer any details. I know she wants me to ask her why she's not well. She craves attention more than anyone I've ever known. That's what irritates me about her. I consider our past and then consider whether she ever views anything that has happened between us with any sentiment. I doubt it.

I sip my beer and watch Eli converse with an older couple he apparently knows. Eli isn't the same person I once knew. We used to be best friends, but now he acts completely detached from everyone. I suspect that the strained relationship he had with his father may be partly to blame. Eli always had the intellect and the drive to be whatever he wanted, but sometimes when we were younger I would notice that he never appeared to really enjoy himself like the rest of us. One time when I asked him if something was wrong, he said he felt hollow inside.

Before I leave Wayside, I place a few dollars on the bar for Eli. I don't have the energy to ask him if he's OK. I pause beside my car and send Scarlett a text message that says, "I miss you." I get into my car. I put the key in the ignition, but I don't start the vehicle. Instead I sit and think about Scarlett. I don't know if she'll say yes to my proposal. I guess I should be more concerned about it than I actually am. I don't even know if we are good for one another. I never understood how people can promise anything forever. I start my car.

***

Ryah opens her front door. She's wearing a tight white tank top that reveals that she isn't wearing bra. Her bright-blue shorts are so tiny they make her legs look longer. It's a tragedy that such a beautiful girl is always so sad.

"Come in," she whispers. Her hair looks like it hasn't been washed in a few days.

"I can't stay long," I convey as she closes the door. She doesn't appear surprised.

"It's OK. I didn't expect that you would," she says in an unaffected tone. "Do you want anything to drink?"

"I shouldn't be here," I blurt, ignoring her question. Ryah's expression changes to curiosity. She stands motionless, not knowing what I'm about to say. "But I can't deny my feelings for you."

Ryah smiles and takes a few slow steps toward me. "I'm sorry I said those terrible things to you before. I have been so confused," she says. She reaches for me. I feel her fingertips pressing on my forearm. She pulls me closer to her while looking up into my eyes.

"I came here because…"

Ryah hugs me loosely. I can feel her hands run the length of my back. She stops at my waist and takes a step backward, away from me.

"I thought I should tell you that this past weekend I went to my parents…" Ryah looks at me and offers a devious smile. She slowly begins to undo my belt. I look down. "It's just that I am confused too, and hurt…" Her hands keep working until my belt is dangling loosely from my pants. I take a deep breath. She unbuttons my pants and opens the zipper. I can feel myself shaking. "Ryah…"

Ryah's hands are still gripping my open pants. She looks up at me, still smiling. "Yes, Bo. What is it?"

The desire is overwhelming. I shouldn't have visited her. She waits for me to speak. "Don't stop," I beg. She kisses my lips and then my neck. I want to be a different person.

CHAPTER FORTY-FOUR
A Mother's Love

Ryah Klein

As we sit in the living room of the house I grew up in, my mother eyes me with the same look of disapproval I've experienced for as long as I can remember. I keep waiting for a time when her expression loses its impact on me, but so far that hasn't happened. She makes me feel like a piece of chewing gum stuck to the bottom of her shoe. I don't think my mother ever forgave me. She probably still believes I'm to blame for everything that happened with my stepfather. I believe she loved me less after that whole episode, if she still loves me at all. At times I think my love for her has been completely extinguished as a result of the way she has treated me. My mother excuses herself to make some hot tea. I watch her walk to the kitchen. Her house smells like potpourri. I want to scream. While I wait, I look out the window and watch a brown squirrel dangle from a low branch while munching on an acorn. She returns and hands me a mug of tea before warning me that it's very hot. Her patronizing face disgusts me. I watch the steam rise from the tea and envy the way it disappears. I want to vanish into thin air too. I don't know why I'm here.

"You look tired," she says as I blow on my tea.

I look at her. "Thanks."

"Are you getting enough sleep? I haven't heard from you in over a month. Don't tell me you're having problems with another guy. You really need to settle down, Ryah. You're twenty-eight years old. You need to find a good man."

"There's no such thing as a good man, Mother." I'm glaring at her now.

"That's part of your problem. You're way too pessimistic. Men don't like depressed girls. I swear your cynicism is going to leave you a very lonely woman if you're not careful." She sips her tea as if I should interpret her put-downs as advice.

"I don't need a man." I look away from her and stare out the window. The squirrel isn't in the tree any longer.

"So you've already given up on living a normal, decent life? For God's sake, Ryah, you have to quit jumping from one dysfunctional relationship to the next. Don't you want a family? I pray every night that you find someone who will love you and take care of you." I look at her again. Her blue pants are perfectly pressed, and the white button-down blouse she's wearing stops right at her waistline. Even her posture is without a flaw. *Does she ever relax?*

"You don't get it," I say after an extended pause.

She sets her cup of tea on the small end table beside her chair. "What don't I get?" she asks in a condescending tone.

"It's not that I can't find a man that loves me. There are plenty of men who love me. The issue is I don't love them. And I don't need a man to take care of me."

She sighs audibly. "If you say so. That sounds like a pretty lonely existence to me, though."

"Why do you care so goddamn much? It's not your life." A growing hatred within me becomes impossible to ignore.

"Ryah! Don't use that language in this house."

"I shouldn't have come." I set my mug on the floor beside my chair and stand up.

"What are you doing?" she asks in a frantic voice.

"I'm leaving. What does it look like I'm doing?" I walk to the door.

"Ryah!" my mother shouts. I open the door. "Ryah, I didn't mean to upset you. Calm down."

I turn around to face her and find that she's standing right behind me. "You didn't mean to upset me with all this talk about how I'm fucking up my life and how I'm a worthless person? Really? Is this your idea of a healthy conversation between mother and daughter? You're so concerned about appearances that you forget that maybe I just need your support without the constant criticism. Maybe I need you to accept me for who I am."

The expression on her face is a combination of surprise and terror. "Ryah, I only want what is best for you," she whimpers. I turn away from her and walk out the door. "Ryah!" she screams. When I stop and face her, I see that she's crying while standing in the doorway. "Don't do this. Please come back and talk to me," she pleads.

I can't look at her any longer. I hear her sobbing as I walk away.

CHAPTER FORTY-FIVE
Going Nowhere

Kasey Price

Tyler and Nick keep buying me drinks at Wayside. My reluctance to join them doesn't deter their efforts. They insist that I drink with them. I haven't been happy in a long while, and my friends decided that I needed a night out because they said they were tired of my sulking. I take a shot of tequila Nick places in front of me and chase it with beer. Tyler nudges my arm and directs my attention to a middle-aged blonde sitting across the bar. This is going to be a long night.

I can't stop thinking about how I ruined it with Franki. She is the only girl in this entire town worth chasing, and somehow I managed to lose her. I may never find another girl like Franki, and that depresses me.

"What about that one?" Tyler asks. I can barely hear him over the music. Eli looks at me from behind the bar and nods while smiling. I raise my glass of beer to salute him.

I lean closer to Tyler. "What about her?"

"Never mind. We have the whole night. We'll find you a girl to get your mind off Ryah." I haven't thought about Ryah much lately. Ever since I told Franki that Eli was seeing Ryah, I've tried to forget my involvement with her.

"What's she like?" Nick asks before he takes a swig from his beer.

"What's who like?" I ask. Nick and Tyler laugh.

"Ryah," Nick replies.

I look at Nick and then Tyler. "What do you mean?"

They look at each other before Nick says, "Come on, man. What's she like? She has to be great in bed."

"Wait a second, Nick. Haven't you messed around with her before?" Tyler asks. I feel sick.

"Did I?"

"Remember Pete's party during the winter break of our freshman year of college when everyone was back in town? Ryah was wearing that thin shirt you could see through after that dumbass Tony spilled his beer on her?"

"Oh yeah. Shit, I almost forgot about that night. Damn, she was looking good too," Nick recalls. None of what they're saying surprises me. "I don't think we did much," he continues.

"What do you mean, you didn't do much? She was all about you that night. You two were upstairs for hours."

"She wanted to, I think, but I was too drunk. She begged me to stay upstairs with her because she said she couldn't go home. She mentioned something about her stepdad being there and blah, blah, blah. I don't know the rest."

Nick and Tyler forget their initial question to me, and I don't offer a reminder. Nick orders another round of tequila shots, and we all take them together. The more shots we drink, the easier they go down. I get the feeling that Eli is watching me. *Does he know I talked to Franki about him?*

Nick is standing by the jukebox, dancing as he selects songs from the playlist. Tyler is over talking to the middle-aged blonde, who screams, "Yeah!" every time a new song plays. I'm still sitting at the bar drinking beer. Periodically I'll watch an old man who is smoking and drinking whiskey straight. He keeps nodding off and almost burning his own arm with the lit end of the cigarette. Just before the cigarette touches his skin, he snaps awake and takes a puff. He doesn't appear to notice anyone else in the bar, or maybe he just doesn't care.

Tyler is busy kissing the blonde, and Nick is trying to score drugs from anyone who will listen. There's nothing left for me here any longer. I've lost everything, and here I sit at Wayside getting drunk. Eli walks over to me. I don't know whether to be suspicious or to act like I don't know who he is. As he approaches, he smiles.

"You're Kasey Price, right?" he asks in a friendly voice.

"Yeah, that's right," I confirm, still not sure what to expect.

"I'm Eli. I've seen you around before. I grew up here, but I just recently returned to town." He extends his hand to shake mine. His grip is firm.

"It's nice to meet you."

"Likewise," he says. His disposition is confident but not arrogant. If I didn't know he was cheating on Franki, I'd probably like him. "Are you celebrating something tonight?"

"Not really. My friends wanted me to come out for some drinks."

"It looks like they are enjoying themselves." Eli chuckles. I look over and see Tyler rubbing the blonde's leg as he talks into her ear.

"I'm sure you see quite a bit in here."

"I don't mind it. It's difficult to have any privacy in a small town," he imparts.

"You are right about that." I suddenly feel uncomfortable. I finish my beer.

"Let me get you another one," Eli offers.

"It's OK. I better get these two out of here before they defile themselves any more than they already have."

"They're fine. This one is on the house," he insists. He takes my glass and walks to the tap to fill it.

I don't know what to think of him. When he returns, I thank him.

"No problem, man. Don't mention it."

Eli empties some ashtrays and collects a few empty glasses but doesn't stray far from me.

"Do you think you'll stay in Payne, or are you planning to move away again?" I finally ask.

"Well, my father passed not too long ago, so now I own Wayside. I've thought about selling the business and starting over where no one knows me, but I don't know if that would help at all, you know? Plus, my girlfriend works in town, and I don't think she would want to move away anytime soon." Eli hasn't stopped smiling since he started talking to me.

"That makes sense." I take a drink and start planning my exit. I know at the very least Eli has most likely heard about me from Franki, and at the very most he knows that I told her that he's having an affair with Ryah. I find Eli's cavalier manner disturbing. I start looking around the bar to avoid eye contact. I expect him to mention Franki's name at any moment. My thoughts are racing. *What do I say if he asks if I dated Franki? What do I do if he confronts me about telling her about his affair with Ryah? How do I get out of here?*

Suddenly, without saying anything, Eli walks away and starts taking money out of the tip jar and organizing it into piles right next to the cash register. I seize the opportunity and walk over to Tyler, who is so drunk he's slurring.

"Let's go, man. I need to get some sleep," I say just as the blonde yells, "I love this song."

"Come on, Kasey. Aren't you having fun?"

CHAPTER FORTY-SIX
I Never Thought I Would

Franki Rose

I am a good person. All I want out of life is to be happy. But I am so tired of doing the right thing when everyone around me only seems to take advantage of me. I want to be appreciated for who I really am, not who other people want me to be. *Is that even possible?* Sometimes I don't make any sense.

I'm wearing the orange-and-red bracelet on my left wrist. I haven't taken it off since John bought it for me. Eli hasn't even commented on it. *Has he noticed? Does he even care?* I watch John walking down the sidewalk as I sit on the steps of St. John's Cathedral. His hair looks messy, but in a good way. He's wearing a light-blue button-up shirt with no shirt underneath. The top three buttons are undone so that his smooth chest is exposed. His jeans look old and have frayed hems that hang over his black boots. John smiles when he sees me and offers a shy wave.

"How are you?" John asks. His dark-brown eyes sparkle in the sunlight.

"I'm doing well. How are you?" I try to look cute, but instead I'm sure I look like a dork.

"I can't complain. This weather has been so nice. You look absolutely beautiful." He hasn't stopped looking at me.

"Why thank you." I perform a slight curtsy, which causes him to laugh.

"Would you like to walk with me?"

"I would love to." I have butterflies in my stomach and my mouth is dry.

I periodically glance at John playfully as we walk. When he looks at me, I turn away. He nudges my arm.

"You can never have enough cats," I blurt.

He laughs. "What?"

"Think about it. It's true."

We stop at a yogurt place and I order a red raspberry yogurt waffle cone. John gets his yogurt in a bowl and proceeds to watch me make a mess of myself as we sit at a table outside. Yogurt collects around my lips, and I purposefully act like I don't know it's there. John starts laughing, and I say, "What?"

"You're hilarious."

I reply with, "I have no idea what you're talking about," before I take a bite out of the cone. The yogurt runs down my hand. I don't know why I am acting so goofy, other than it feels good to have fun.

"Let's go to my place and listen to music," John suggests.

"Will there be some harmonica?"

"Of course."

"Let's do it!"

While we walk to John's apartment, I think of Eli writing our names on the bridge. He hasn't talked to me much at all since we returned from our weekend trip. I feel John tap me on the shoulder.

"This is for you." He is holding an orange carnation.

"Where did you get that?"

"I plucked it for you from that person's yard."

"You can't steal people's flowers!" I exclaim as I giggle.

"It's not a crime to share a flower."

John's apartment is messy, just like mine. He has mismatched paintings hanging in his living room. One is of a grazing horse. Another is of an autumn sky. They amuse me. John goes to the kitchen to pour us some white wine. When he returns with the two glasses, he finds me messing with his stereo.

"I can't figure it out," I admit.

"It's OK." He hands me a glass and then turns on a melodic tune complete with a harmonica intro that makes my neck go limp as my eyes close.

"Do you like it?"

I open my eyes. "The music?"

"Yes."

"I'm in love with it." I close my eyes again. I can almost feel every emotion at once.

John asks, "What do you want out of life?"

"To be happy?"

"Is that a question or a statement?"

I'm lying on the floor, holding my flower while humming to the music. John lies beside me. I can feel him looking at me. I turn my head. It happens in slow motion. He leans in, and his lips touch mine, softly at first, and then with more force. I don't resist. I like it. John kisses me again. I feel so alive. He reaches for me. His touch causes time to stop as his fingers comb through my hair. I can't hear the music any longer.

John's hand moves to my thigh, and I suddenly become aware of what I'm doing. Eli would die if he knew. Intense guilt replaces the pleasure. I stop kissing John.

"What's the matter?"

"I can't do this," I confess.

"What…why?"

"I just can't." I look at the ceiling.

"You didn't have a problem with this a second ago. What changed?"

I turn my head to look at John. He appears angry. "I'm sorry."

"That's all you're going to say?"

"What else can I say?" I sit up so that I'm looking down at John. I don't want him to be upset with me.

"Nothing." He stands up and moves to the couch. He is sitting and staring straight ahead at nothing in particular.

"John, I'm having such a good time."

"You're not acting like you're having a good time."

"Please, John."

"Don't please, John me."

"What do you want from me? Do you want me to leave?" John doesn't say anything. "John...do you want me to leave?" I repeat.

"You probably should."

I start to cry. "I can't believe this." I feel like I'm in a nightmare.

"I can't believe *you*," he says in a cold voice. I don't understand how he transformed so quickly.

I walk toward the door slowly, expecting that John will stop me. He doesn't. I pause with my hand on the doorknob. I can hear him mumbling something. I turn around. He doesn't look like the same person I met at the sidewalk festival.

"Go," he commands in a loud voice.

The tears won't stop. *What did I do wrong?*

CHAPTER FORTY-SEVEN
Buried Answers

Elijah Noor

He must have cared. I mean, I have seen pictures of him holding me when I was a young child. He didn't appear to resent me then. In fact, I like to think that the expression on my father's face in those pictures indicates pride. When my mother's illness started getting worse and she suddenly became noncommunicative, he started treating me differently. It's as if her illness became his illness. Eventually she could no longer live with us. He visited her dutifully at first. His visits tapered as her condition worsened, until he quit going altogether. His disappointment in life manifested into a distraction from it. He turned to the very thing he hated: God. Meanwhile, I could never do well enough. My father's criticisms cut me down gradually until I shut down entirely. I have experienced periods of understanding what others feel, but I never thought of myself as real.

His headstone is a simple one that sits flush with the ground. All that is etched into the stone are his name and the year of his birth, followed by the year of his death. My mother is buried in another section of the cemetery, beside her parents. My maternal grandparents never liked my father. In their opinion, my father never allowed my mother to fulfill her potential. She had a full scholarship to attend law school, but she became pregnant with me shortly after finishing her bachelor's degree and decided that she would stay home with me while my father ran Wayside. My mother's parents never forgave my father for that, even when the business became a thriving local restaurant. I look down at his stone and read it once, and then I read it again.

Weeds surround his marker. I kneel down and pull a few of the taller ones from the ground. He never forgave me. I don't even know what I did. I became more aware of his contempt for me as I grew older. He quit trying to conceal it after I ended my relationship with Scarlett. I couldn't tell him why I ended it with her. It hurt too badly to verbalize what had happened. *How do you tell your father that the woman you love aborted your child without your consent?* Right after it happened, I wanted to disappear. I wanted to not feel any longer. For the first time in my life, I quit caring about whether or not my father approved of me. I think he quit caring too. It's easier not to care.

Now that my father is gone, it has become nearly impossible to remember him as he truly was. I never understood him. Maybe that's why I don't understand myself. None of that matters now. I hear a few cars drive slowly by the cemetery. I consider walking over to my mother's grave but decide I should go home instead. I shouldn't have come here. My phone vibrates in my pocket. It's Ryah texting me again. I don't respond. *What is left to say?*

I stand and look around the cemetery. There's no one around. I don't know what compelled me to visit my father's grave. I don't think I'll return. I mean, what's the point? It's not going to make him love me. A breeze causes my shirt to cling to my chest. I watch as the few remaining weeds around his marker sway in the wind. I can feel my eyes tearing up. I can't remember the last time I shed a tear. The sun shines bright overhead, but it's not hot. I feel my phone vibrate in my pocket again. This time I don't check to see who is trying to contact me. I don't want anyone to know I'm here. I look down at his name one last time and then walk away. Another gust of wind causes a few leaves to fall from the trees as I'm walking to my car. I stop and watch them float to the ground. I can't explain why I end up hating anyone who loves me. A question repeats over and over in my mind. *Who will pull the weeds from my grave?*

CHAPTER FORTY-EIGHT
Plastic Flowers

Ryah Klein

T he problem with artificial flowers is that they're always in bloom. I consider that as I stare at the plastic daisy positioned in the wine bottle on my table. My agony is real, but I try to tell myself that all the worry and concern will be worth it someday. Eli is supposed to visit tonight, but he hasn't answered any text messages. *What can he be doing?* I feel uneasy. I can't stop pacing. Tonight is the night when I plan to tell him what I should have told him the first time I saw him at the café. I have to tell him. I need to be with him.

I've considered all the potential problems he may cite as reasons why we can't be together. I know he has issues with trust, but so do I. I believe our problems can be overcome with time if we can simply keep other people from interrupting our closeness. If only we could be alone, I mean truly alone, then there would be no way he could deny that what we have is special. And then there's Franki.

I hear a car engine idling outside and rush to the window to see if it's Eli. It is. I am so worked up I feel nauseous. I can't breathe. I hurry to the bathroom and check my hair in the mirror. I look at my reflection and take a deep breath. I would have never thought that a man could cause me to be this way. Suddenly I can't remember the words I had rehearsed in my mind all day. *What will I say to Eli? How will I even broach the subject of us being together? Should I even expose my inner feelings in this way? Will my honesty turn him off? What if he doesn't feel the same way?*

I open the door to find Eli looking forlorn. He doesn't say anything as he walks by me and into my apartment. I close the door behind him. I don't know why he is in a bad mood, but I wish that he wasn't, especially tonight.

"Is something wrong?" I ask carefully. He doesn't respond immediately. Maybe he's tired.

"It's nothing," he says in a quiet voice.

"Are you sure?"

"I don't want to talk about it."

"Come on in and have a seat. Would you like something to drink?" I walk to the kitchen but stop and turn to look at him because he doesn't respond. I've never seen Eli look this way. He looks completely lost. I'm somehow moved by his apparent sadness and want nothing more than to please him. *How does a woman care for a man?*

"What?" he asks once he snaps out of his trance.

"Would you like something to drink? I have water or beer."

"I'll have a beer."

"OK." I walk to the kitchen. I open the fridge and hold the door open longer than necessary. The cool air rushes out and soothes me. I take a deep breath and feel revitalized. I shut the refrigerator door. *I can do this. I will do this.* I open the beer and walk back to the living room.

"Listen, Ryah. I can't stay long," Eli insists as I hand him the beer.

"Why is that? I was hoping—"

"I've had a bad day," Eli interrupts.

"I'm sorry."

"It's not your fault."

"I was hoping to talk to you about something," I begin. Eli takes a drink of the beer and then sets the bottle on my end table.

"I need to talk to you too," Eli asserts. My stomach drops. "Can I sit down?"

"Sure," I say, uncertain what Eli needs to tell me. He sits on my couch, and I sit beside him. I don't want to be too far from him, because then I'll lose my courage to be honest with him.

"So what would you like to talk about?" Eli asks in a distracted manner.

"Would you prefer we wait, since you've had a bad day?" I ask. Part of me hopes he says yes so I don't have to continue.

"It's OK, Ryah. I've had a lot on my mind lately is all."

I look at Eli. I see my reflection in his eyes and hope he sees his reflection in mine. He looks gorgeous, even when in despair. "I want to tell you something that I feel strongly about, but I'm scared," I admit.

"Why are you scared?"

"I don't want you to hate me. I don't want to feel rejected."

"I'll never hate you, Ryah. We've been through quite a bit together."

I smile. "OK. Well…" I pause. "Eli…" I stop again.

"What is it?" He looks genuinely concerned.

"You know that I like you, right?"

"Yes. In fact, that's what I came here to talk to you about," he confesses.

"Really?"

"Yes."

I smirk. I feel lighter. "Well, that makes this a little easier," I say.

"Does it?"

"I want to be with you. There, I said it. I want us to be together."

"Ryah—"

"Wait, hear me out about this, OK?"

"But—"

"I know what you're going to say. I've thought about all the issues we will face, and I want you to know that I really believe we can overcome them."

"It's—"

"Please listen. I don't know what's happening to me, but something inside me is changing. For the first time, I can actually feel real emotion.

I care about you. I want to make you happy. I know you will make me happy. God, Eli, I think I am...no. I know I am falling for you, and I can't stop myself. No matter how hard I try to ignore it, I want you. I want to be with you. I want to share my life with you. I want us to be a real couple. I know you never expected this from me. I can't imagine how you view me, but I'm telling you the truth. I want you and only you. That's crazy. I'm crazy. I never thought I could have these feelings. I thought I would feel empty forever. I want to please you. I want all of you. I will do whatever it takes. Believe me, I never expected this. I try so hard not to think of you, but it doesn't work. Lately I find myself thinking about us and what we've shared so far. I think about what we have yet to experience together, and it makes me smile." I pause when I notice Eli's expression is blank. "Should I regret telling you this?"

"Ryah, what have we done?" he asks while looking into my eyes.

"What do you mean? Eli, I just exposed my soul to you, and that's how you respond?"

"What about Franki, Ryah? Have you completely forgotten about your friend who I am seeing? What about her? Do you know how devastated she would be if she ever found out about us? We can't do that to her."

"We're not doing anything to her. We can't help that we have feelings for one another. She's not perfect. Franki still talks to Kasey."

"I know that. He's been telling her that I'm sleeping with you."

"Kasey is pathetic. He's always been weak."

"I don't think this is a good idea at all." Eli leans back and closes his eyes after he speaks. He takes a deep breath and exhales audibly.

"What's wrong with you? Don't you feel what I feel?"

"Everything is wrong with me. We can't do this to Franki. We've gone too far."

"I'll talk to her, Eli. Everything will work out. She'll listen to me once she realizes that I've changed and that I really have feelings for you. I can't believe you're being this way."

"Franki is supposed to be your best friend."

"She is."

"I can't do this."

"What? You can't do what?" I demand.

"This! I can't commit to knowingly damaging someone like Franki. She doesn't deserve it."

"Goddamn. You really still believe Franki is an innocent sweetheart, don't you? You poor bastard."

"What? Why do you say that?"

"You really don't know? I thought if anyone could see through her bullshit, it would be you."

"Quit fucking around, Ryah. Jesus, not everyone is like us."

"Have you met John?"

"John?"

"You heard me. Haven't you noticed her new bracelet?" I can tell Eli's mind is trying to outwork mine. "Perfect Franki went on a date with John. She thought he wasn't like other guys. She thought he wasn't like you. She's so naïve sometimes. Then when he wanted to fuck her, she said no and he kicked her frigid ass out of his place. You haven't heard this story?" I ask in a sarcastic tone. "Didn't you find it strange that she started wearing that hideous bracelet and then suddenly took it off?"

"She said she lost it."

"Oh, she did. She lost it when she threw it on the sidewalk as she ran out of John's place crying her eyes out. Do you still think she's pure? Do you still want to protect her?"

"You're lying."

"Why would I? I have nothing to gain by making up that story. Franki is my friend, remember?"

"You're cruel."

"The truth hurts, doesn't it?"

"She would…" Eli stops before he finishes.

"She would what? Never do that? She did do just that. Maybe you should ask her if you don't believe me."

"It doesn't matter," he says.

"Why doesn't it matter, Eli? Have you finally awakened from your denial? We can only trust each other."

"Is that what you think?"

"Listen, I'm sorry you had to find this out from me, but at least you know. Don't be angry with me for being honest with you."

"I'm not angry with you."

I lean over and kiss his lips. He doesn't kiss me back. I pull away and look at him and try again. This time I grab the back of his head and kiss him forcefully. He kisses me back aggressively. His right hand grabs my breast and squeezes it so hard that it hurts. I keep kissing him. His hand moves to my leg and then my inner thigh. I pull his hair. I can feel his fingers probing inside my shorts, and then he abruptly stops and pushes me away.

"Stop. Just fucking stop," Eli shouts.

"What?" I kiss him again, but he pushes me away. "What do you want? Do you want me to suck your cock? Tell me what you want and I'll do it."

"I want you to…" Eli stops talking and stands up.

"Where are you going? What do you want?" I plead as I scramble to my feet.

"Nothing, Ryah. It's over."

"What are you talking about?" I beg, almost crying. Eli moves to the front door and opens it. I start sobbing uncontrollably. "What did I do?" I yell. "Please don't leave me!" Eli looks at me and then walks out. I don't think I ever mattered to him.

CHAPTER FORTY-NINE
New Beginning

Kasey Price

Sometimes when everything is going wrong, it's easier to start over. That's where I am in my life. There's nothing left for me in Payne. The people I have known for years have changed. I have changed too. We're familiar strangers now. I need to go somewhere where my past won't hinder my future. I daydream about being reborn into the person I want to be. I can change. I just need a chance.

My phone sounds with an incoming text while I'm in my bedroom packing the clothes in my closet into boxes. I check and see that it's Franki. I'm surprised she answered. I sent her a text earlier to tell her that I'm moving to Chicago. I didn't think she would respond. She asks if she can come over. I tell her I'll be packing all day and she's welcome anytime. She says she'll be over in ten minutes. I turn my phone off after her last text. I haven't told anyone else I'm leaving. Franki is the only one worth saying good-bye to.

Franki's knock startles me. I stick the photos I was looking at inside a book sitting by my bed and walk to the living room to invite her in.

"Please excuse the mess," I say as soon as I open the door and see Franki standing in front of me wearing jeans and a purple hooded sweatshirt. She has cut the neck of the sweatshirt so that it hangs on her loosely. I can't get over how good she looks.

"I can't believe you're leaving," she says while she looks around at all the boxes littering my living room.

"I can't either. I'm excited."

"Wow," is all Franki says.

"Do you want to talk to me while I pack?" I ask. Franki finally directs her attention toward me.

"Sure."

I lead Franki to my bedroom. I have about finished packing the clothes in my closet. I notice Franki standing in the doorway. I wonder if she's thinking about all the nights we shared together in this room.

"You have a lot of clothes," she blurts.

"I know. I forgot I had some of these shirts."

"I have to ask, Kasey. Why are you leaving? It's not because of..."

"Oh, no. It's not because of us. I need to apologize for the way I've behaved."

"No, you don't."

"Yes, I do. I'm embarrassed. I guess I liked me when I was with you. But I hurt you and I'm truly sorry for that. I understand why our relationship had to end. You couldn't trust me. I still feel horrible about that."

"I forgave you, Kasey."

"I know you did. That makes me feel even worse, because I don't deserve your forgiveness."

"Oh, stop it. We'll always be friends," she says in the sweetest voice.

"I believe so too, Franki."

"So if you're not leaving because of us, why are you leaving?"

"I need a fresh start. I don't really know anyone here except you."

She appears puzzled. "Yes, you do. You know everyone I know."

"I've learned that I don't really know them and they don't really know me. We've all changed."

"I guess we have. So why Chicago?"

"Because I've had enough of small towns. Everyone meddles in everyone else's lives."

Franki nods. "It does get old. Why do you think that happens in small towns?"

"Boredom," I say without hesitation. "I don't know why else. I need to move somewhere where I can be anonymous."

Franki pauses before she says, "I don't know what that would be like. I don't know that I'd like it."

"Why not?" I press.

"I don't know. It sounds kind of scary, going where nobody knows you."

"It's the same as Payne, only in the city people don't pretend they care."

"Pretend?"

"Yes. Pretend. Have you ever considered how much terrible shit happens here? I mean, once you penetrate the boring small-town surface."

"I guess I haven't." Franki's stare becomes unfocused.

"I suppose it's easier to be nice to strangers," I say. Franki doesn't respond. "What plagues people is not those who don't love them, but those who do," I continue. "Don't you think?"

"I don't know. You may be right," she replies. Her face appears to lose some color.

"Are you all right?" Franki doesn't say anything. "Franki?"

"Yeah. Sorry."

"Are you feeling OK?"

"Yes. I'm just sad. I'll miss you."

"I'm moving, not dying. You can visit me. It would do you well to get away."

"Yeah. That might be fun."

"You might even be able to drag me to a museum."

Franki giggles. "A museum?" she asks, still chuckling. "You would have to be pretty desperate for a visitor before I would expect that to happen."

"Anything is possible."

"Except that," she says jokingly. "I'm serious, Kasey. I'm going to miss you. When are you leaving?"

"I'm going to miss you too. I'm leaving next Sunday."

"Can I see you before you leave?"

"We'll see. I'm not too fond of good-byes."

"I hate them," Franki admits.

"Me too. So maybe we shouldn't say good-bye."

"Kasey, can I ask you something?" Franki suddenly sounds very serious.

"Sure," I say with a hint of dread in my voice.

"Remember what you said about Eli?"

"Yes. I don't want to be involved, though. That's between you two. I'm sorry I even brought it up. It's just that I hate to see—"

"Is it true?" Franki asks in a solemn voice.

"Franki, I don't really want to get involved."

"Is it true, Kasey?"

CHAPTER FIFTY
Nothing New

Scarlett Davison

I sit down with a glass of Chardonnay and the romance novel I just started and can't put down. I hear a car pull into my driveway. I get up to see who it is. I am surprised when I see Eli walking toward my house. I'm actually glad to see him. I'll never be completely over him. I know I shouldn't admit that.

I open the door before Eli knocks. He offers a forced smile, which usually indicates that he is overwhelmed, or plotting against someone.

"Come in, Eli. How are you?" I ask politely. Maybe I should hate him, but I don't. He walks inside without saying a word. "What's going on?" I continue as I close the door.

"I came here to tell you something," he declares in a shaky voice.

"Is something wrong?"

"Yes."

"What?"

"Do you have any coffee? I haven't slept much."

"I can make some," I say with some hesitation. "What do you need to tell me?"

"It's about Bo," he answers. "I don't know if you should be with him any longer."

"Wait. Before you say anything, have you heard something about him?" I'm worried Eli has heard that Bo proposed to me.

"I didn't hear something about him. I know something about him that I need to tell you." Eli fidgets with his phone.

"OK. Let me start the coffee." I walk into the kitchen, and while I prepare the coffee, I try to consider what Eli is about to tell me. I can't think of what it could be, which makes me nervous. I reenter the living room.

"It should be ready in a few minutes," I tell Eli. He slides his phone inside the front pocket of his dark-blue jeans.

"I want you to know that I don't want to hurt you," he begins. "I say that because what I need to tell you is not going to be what you want to hear, but you need to hear it."

I want to sit down, but I don't want Eli to know that I'm anxious. "Go ahead."

"Bo is cheating on you." Eli studies my reaction after he reveals this to me. I don't offer much of one.

"I know," I say with nonchalance.

"What? You know?" Eli's baffled expression amuses me.

"Yes, I know he's cheating. I'm not naïve, Eli. You should know that."

"I don't think you're naïve. So you know about Ryah?"

"Is that her name? I didn't know who he was cheating with, but I knew he was cheating."

Eli shakes his head in disbelief. "You don't care?"

"Should I?"

"I would think so, since you're with him."

"I don't know why I'm with him." The truth is I'm with Bo because I can't be with Eli, but I don't tell him that.

"I don't understand you, Scarlett. Why would you ever let someone like Bo use you like this?"

"Aren't you friends with Bo?"

"Are you serious, Scarlett? Bo? He's a self-absorbed idiot." Eli's disgust is apparent.

"Why do you associate with him then?" I pry. I enjoy shifting the emphasis from me to Eli. I've only seen him squirm like this a few times since I've known him.

"What do you want me to say? It's a small town. Everything isn't how it appears."

I smile. I don't know why I'm enjoying this so much. "You would really hate to know what Bo is up to."

"What? He's such a goddamn simpleton."

"I shouldn't tell you. It's not that big of a deal." I almost want to laugh at Eli's frustration.

"Don't do this. Don't fucking start something and then not finish. What were you going to tell me?"

I stare at Eli. I can tell he's getting angry. Maybe he cares about me after all. "He proposed to me."

Eli takes a step toward me. "Are you fucking serious?"

"Yes."

"What did you say?" There's desperation in Eli's voice. His confidence has deflated considerably.

"Why? Do you care?"

Eli looks at my hand, searching for a ring that isn't there. "Fuck it. I'm leaving. This is ridiculous. You're pissing me off." Eli turns from me and walks toward the door.

"Wait," I call to him. He stops and turns around. "Don't get all upset, Eli."

"Don't get upset? Really?"

"I told Bo I had to think about it."

Eli's whole demeanor changes immediately. "You're thinking about it? At least you didn't say yes," he says with some relief.

"Come here," I say as I walk to him and hug him. He doesn't hug me back initially, but slowly his arms envelop me. I rest my head against his.

Eli pulls his head away from mine so that he can look down at me. "Are you seriously considering marrying Bo?" he asks in a calmer voice.

"I don't want to talk about Bo right now." Eli's arms fall from me. He takes a step back.

"Did you ever tell me that you missed me when you didn't mean it?" he asks.

CHAPTER FIFTY-ONE
Friendly Advice

Bo Schnep

No moment reveals a person's love for another more than the moment right before that person is unfaithful. I felt my love for Scarlett every time I was about to be with Ryah, but that didn't stop me. I wish that it had. *God, why didn't it? What's wrong with me?* I wanted too much. *Isn't that normal?* No matter what I do, I can't change what happened. *Why can't Scarlett understand that I'm sorry? Why can't she forgive me? How did she find out?*

I pace in the living room of my house before I decide I need to go somewhere. Once I'm in my car, I become painfully aware that I have nowhere to go. I can't lose Scarlett. I decide that there's only one person who can possibly help. I don't want to ask for a favor, but what else can I do? I'm desperate. I now know what is important. I only hope that it's not too late.

I see a light on as I approach the house. Questions flood my mind. *What if he's not alone? What if I make a fool of myself? What if he can't help?* I park my car along the street and take a deep breath. I turn the engine off and step out of my vehicle. It's a cool night and the sky is clear. Stars shine bright overhead. I look up at them and consider how distant they are. I want everything to return to the way it was. *Will I still think of Ryah if Scarlett forgives me? Will I still go to Ryah when I'm feeling lonely?* I will have to tell Ryah that it's over. I can't ever see her again. Even if she tries to contact me, I can't respond. That will be difficult. She's so beautiful. I keep reminding myself that there's something about Ryah that is horribly broken. If only Ryah were a different person.

I knock on the front door and listen for movement inside. I hear footsteps approaching. I feel a rush of relief when Eli opens the door. I can't disguise my discomfort. He detects it right away.

"What's wrong, Bo? You look like you're ill."

"I am. Can I speak to you? I've done something horrible, and I need a friend. I know it's late, but you're the only one I can trust," I announce in a rush of words that fall from my mouth all at once.

"Please, come on in." Eli moves to the side to let me inside his house. I stand in the entranceway until he closes the door. "Have a seat," he urges while motioning with his hand toward a chair in his living room. I lumber toward the chair and sit on the edge. "Tell me what's going on."

"I don't know where to start. I've really done it this time."

"It's OK," he assures me. "Tell me what happened."

"Scarlett left me. She says she's going to move away. I didn't know who else to go to." My hands are shaking.

"Scarlett left you?" Eli moves a chair so that it's facing me and sits down.

"Yes," I mutter. I can hear my voice crack. I feel like a fool telling Eli my problems. He's always so strong. Nothing ever bothers him.

"Do you know why?"

"I don't want any of what I'm about to say to leave this house," I plead. "Nobody knows."

Eli nods. "I understand. You have my word," he promises.

"I'm sorry. I'm a mess. I don't know what to do."

"Well, let's see if we can't figure out a solution. It's never too late to correct a mistake," he declares. His confidence actually causes me to feel calmer.

"I cheated on Scarlett, and somehow she found out about it. It was a mistake. God, it was a stupid mistake, and now Scarlett won't even take my calls. She sends me right to voice mail."

"Does she know the person you were with?"

"Yes. It was Ryah Klein," I confess. Eli doesn't offer any sort of reaction. It's as if my news doesn't surprise him in the least.

"So this was what, a one-night stand type thing?"

"Not exactly," I admit.

"Oh…" Eli looks away.

"It's not the way it sounds. I didn't know I had developed such strong feelings for Scarlett until recently. I proposed to her. I want to marry her. And now this comes out and she's left me. I don't know what to do." I lean back after my outburst. Eli is the first person I've been truthful with for longer than I'd like to remember.

"Did you stop seeing Ryah after you proposed?" Eli asks as he leans forward in his chair. His eyes study mine. I suspect he is trying to determine my level of honesty.

"No. I don't know what happened to me. Ryah is…I can't explain it."

Eli reclines in his chair again and takes a deep breath. I wait for him to say something, but he doesn't say anything. The silence is torture.

"I will stop seeing her. I need help getting Scarlett back. She's threatening to move away. She said she doesn't ever want to see me again. She has trust issues, and I betrayed her. What should I do?" I massage the back of my neck. *Why is Eli so quiet?*

"OK. Here's what you need to do," he begins. Eli leans forward and rests his elbows on his thighs while pressing his thumbs to his lips in a dramatic way. "We need to be very methodical about this."

"I agree. Scarlett isn't going to forgive me easily."

"I wouldn't expect so. The first thing you need to do is visit Ryah and tell her that it's over. Can you do that?"

"Yes. Of course."

Eli purses his lips together and clears his throat. "Bo, can you really end this affair with Ryah? If not, maybe you need to just accept that what you had with Scarlett is over. It's obvious to me that if Scarlett does give you a second chance, and that's a substantial *if*, then she will be watching for any deception from you in the future."

"You're right. I've thought about all of that, and I know that I have to end it with Ryah. I want to marry Scarlett," I vow.

"OK. Then you need to visit Ryah tomorrow and explain that your affair with her is over. However, don't say it in those terms. This has to be done carefully. You want Ryah to think that she ended the relationship; that way you can escape this whole ordeal without her feeling resentful."

I am impressed that Eli can be so deceitful. "How do I make Ryah think that she is responsible for ending our relationship?"

"You have to get Ryah to view you as the victim. If she believes she has the position of power, she will automatically feel a sense of superiority that will distort her reason. She will feel the guilt that should be felt by you."

I smile. "That's genius!"

"Bo, I'm actually glad you came to see me tonight. I had planned on visiting you tomorrow," Eli continues.

"Really? Why?"

"Well none of it really made sense until just now. I had intended to ask you about it to see what you thought."

"What are you talking about?" My anxiety returns after only a moment's respite.

"It's about Ryah. I overheard Kasey talking about her in Wayside the other night. I didn't catch everything that he said, but he was with friends and laughing."

"What did he say? Who is Kasey?"

"Kasey Price. Do you know him?" Eli asks.

"I recognize the name. I think I know who he is. What did he say?" The anticipation is excruciating. I feel short of breath.

"He was talking with his friends about how he has been seeing Ryah Klein. I didn't think much about it, but I did hear your name." Eli pauses and studies my reaction.

"He mentioned me? What did he say?"

"Kasey was bragging to his friends about how easy Ryah was and said that you don't even know that he's been seeing her. I didn't know what he meant because I thought you were with Scarlett. I'm sorry, Bo. I had no idea you were seeing Ryah too."

"That motherfucker. He really said that?"

"Yes."

Rage fills me. I can feel my face contort with anger. I want to find Kasey Price and confront him. Eli stands from his chair and walks toward me.

"Calm down, Bo. I'm sorry," he repeats.

"No. It's not your fault. I appreciate you telling me," I reassure him.

"That's why I was going to see you tomorrow. I wanted to see if you could make sense of it, but now it all seems to fit. Bo, you have to promise me you won't do anything stupid. Remember, you need to focus on repairing your relationship with Scarlett. You can't let some guy telling his drunk friends in the bar about how he is fucking your girl behind your back get to you. You don't really care about Ryah. It's Scarlett you love," Eli asserts.

I can't even think, I'm so angry. I stare straight ahead. I can feel my hands tightening into fists.

Eli still stands over me in a protective way. I can tell he is worried about me. "Bo, are you listening to me? Don't do anything foolish. Ryah never cared about you. You have to let it go."

CHAPTER FIFTY-TWO
Bad Habits

Ryah Klein

Bo visited earlier today and told me that he could no longer see me because I have been sleeping with Kasey. I have absolutely no idea who told him. There's no way he could have figured that out by himself. Oh well. I don't really care. Bo told me that he proposed to Scarlett Davison, as if that would in some way upset me. I told him that was nice and then walked inside my apartment and shut the door in his face as he stood there staring at me. He never understood that he was merely a substitute for Eli when Eli wasn't available.

I drive to Wayside to see Eli at the bar. It's past ten in the evening, and I'm hoping that it won't be too busy. Regardless of what Eli said the last time I saw him, I know he cares for me. He wants to push me away. That's what Eli does. He pushes away those who care about him the most because he can't stand to view himself as someone who is worthy of happiness. I know that if I don't give up on him, eventually he'll realize that what we have is unlike anything we've shared with anyone else we've ever been with. Past lovers are reminders of who we once were. My future with Eli is all that concerns me now.

I arrive at Wayside wearing a tight white tank top and jeans that hang low on my hips. I'm not wearing a bra or panties. I need Eli to want me. When I enter the bar, I can hear my black high heels sounding with each step. A few guys are drinking while watching sports on the three televisions that are on. Everyone stops when I walk in the room. They watch me make my way to a seat at the far end of the bar. Their lust is palpable. I hear one of the guys say, "goddamn." It's all so typical. I love when men want me.

Eli looks at me. I smile at him. He walks over slowly. "Hello, Ryah. How are you?" he asks.

"I'm doing well," I say. "How are you?"

"Just fine, thanks. What can I get you?"

I act distracted. I don't want Eli to believe he has any authority over me. I want him to wait. "I'll have a vodka tonic," I say eventually.

"Coming right up." Eli turns and walks to the center of the bar. It's as if he is deliberately trying to treat me like an ordinary customer. *Is he avoiding me?* I take a cigarette from my small purse. I stand from my stool and walk over to some man in his thirties I've never seen before. He's wearing a cliché T-shirt with a bunch of graphics on it. It is too tight for his build. His jeans are old and have a hole in the left knee. He has a stubble beard and is wearing a baseball cap that looks dirty.

"Excuse me," I mouth to him as a song starts to play on the jukebox. He takes one look at me and smiles in a flirtatious way.

"Yes," he replies as he turns his stool to face me.

"Do you have a light?" I ask as I show him the cigarette gripped between my fingers. He immediately digs in the front pocket of his jeans. I look at Eli. He's watching me. When the man retrieves the lighter from his pocket, I put the cigarette to my lips and lean toward him as he flicks the lighter. He lights my cigarette, and I take a slow drag before I pull the cigarette from my lips. I exhale a stream of smoke toward the ceiling. "Thanks." The man doesn't say anything. I saunter back to my seat. I can feel his eyes watching my ass as I walk away.

Eli positions my drink on the bar in front of me but doesn't say anything. I take a drag from my cigarette and blow it in his direction playfully. He walks to the other end of the bar. *He's not still upset about*

Franki, is he? Men always get upset over the wrong women. I finish my drink quickly and motion Eli over. He makes his way to my side of the bar reluctantly. I order another drink. He obliges but doesn't offer any conversation. I don't understand him. I know I look good tonight. The guy who lit my cigarette hasn't taken his eyes off me since I left him. *What is wrong with Eli?*

Eli is annoying me. I don't understand what his problem is. I want to ask him but decide that approach is too direct. He'll become combative. That's how he handles confrontation. I take a pen from my purse and write a note on my napkin that says, "Come over later." I draw a heart underneath it and finish my drink. When he brings me my next drink, I slide the note in his direction. Eli looks down at the napkin on the bar. I watch his eyes as he reads it. He doesn't look up at me and instead wads it into a ball and tosses it in the trash can as he walks away. I want to shout at him and tell him what an asshole he is, but I don't. It's easier to show him what he's missing. I lift my glass from the bar and walk over to the man who lit my cigarette earlier. He's drinking bottled beer. I'm not attracted to him at all, but that won't stop me tonight. One way or another, Eli will want me.

The man wearing the hat introduces himself as Steve when I move to sit by him. He leans into me as he speaks in my ear. I giggle, even though I don't really know what he's saying. I want Eli to hurt as badly as I hurt. I want him to regret every time he has denied me pleasure. I want him to feel something. Steve orders us another round. I feel his hand touch my lower back. When I don't resist, he slides his fingers inside my jeans and feels my bare ass. I lean forward in my seat. It feels good to be touched. Eli brings us the drinks and sees what is happening. I smile at him and then slap Steve's hand away. Steve laughs and says something he intends to be seductive, but instead he sounds moronic. I can see the hate in Eli's eyes. He's helpless. It's a position he's not familiar with. I look Eli in the eyes as Steve slides his hand down the back of my jeans again. This time I don't slap him.

***

Eli hasn't said one word to me since I ordered my first drink, and it's nearing closing time. I'm drunk and horny. I decide that if Eli is going to continue to act like he doesn't care, then maybe he needs to see me leave with another man. I smile while I think of Eli tossing in bed, knowing that another man is enjoying my body. He won't forgive himself for letting me go. Maybe then he'll understand that he cares for me. Steve pays his bill and stands from his stool. I stand up too, leaning on him for balance. He's grabbing my ass forcefully and pulling my body into his. I kiss him on the lips. It's no big deal. I can make myself forget later. Eli watches the whole time but doesn't say anything. As I'm walking out of the bar with Steve, I look back at Eli. Eli's gaze is unfocused. He doesn't look at me. He looks through me. I feel Steve pulling me through the door. I don't want to leave.

CHAPTER FIFTY-THREE
One Last Good-Bye

Kasey Price

I awake from a deep sleep to the sound of what I believe to be my alarm chiming. I rub my eyes and find that it is, luckily, not my alarm. The sound happens again. I pick up my phone to see three new text messages. I'm upset with myself for not silencing my phone before going to bed. Joe is arriving early this morning to help me move to Chicago, and I really need a good night of sleep. I try to close my eyes, but it's too late. The startle caused by the sound of those incoming text messages makes it impossible to fall back asleep. I lie with my eyes open and finally decide to check my phone to see who is texting me at this hour. It's Ryah. The text messages claim, like always, that she is experiencing some sort of crisis. I'm tired. *Why does Ryah text me when she has made it painfully clear that she doesn't care about me?* It's two in the morning.

I remind myself that I need to let go of the past. My phone sounds again. She's begging me to respond. She says she has no one and is so sad that she doesn't know what she will do. The message conveys a level of desperation I don't usually expect from Ryah. Surely she wouldn't harm herself. *Would she?* The more I think about it, the more I realize that I won't be able to live with myself if she does do something impulsive. She needs a friend. I owe it to her to at least do my best to help her.

When I arrive at Ryah's, I find her sitting on the steps of her apartment building with her face buried in her hands. She lifts her head when she hears my car. After I park, I walk to her and immediately notice that she's been crying. Her breathing is heavy and her eyes are red. I've never seen her so distraught. I'm worried. A tear streams down her cheek.

"Thank you," she whimpers.

"Don't thank me, Ryah. You know I care about you. You're going to be all right. I promise. Let's go inside and talk. OK?" She nods and stands. I follow her inside the building. Caring isn't easy.

Once we're inside, Ryah collapses on the couch in her living room. Her place is a mess. I see empty wine bottles and two wineglasses, one with lipstick stains around the rim. Ryah is wearing jeans and a blue tank top. I've never seen her look this disheveled. Even when she's distraught, she's still beautiful. *Why don't women ever recognize their own beauty?*

"What happened?" I ask as I sit beside her on the couch. Ryah begins to sob again. She wraps her arms around me and holds on to me tightly. Her lack of control worries me. I hug her back. She takes a deep breath.

"I…I don't know what to do. I have no one…Eli…God, I'm so stupid." She loosens her grip. She's a shell of her former self.

"Don't say these things. Tell me what's going on. It's going to be OK. Just calm down."

"It's not going to be OK, Kasey. Nothing is OK. Everything is fucked. Don't you understand? I don't know how to love. I don't know how to be loved. If that's not hell, I don't know what is."

"What happened?" I repeat.

"He doesn't care about me. It makes sense. I don't deserve anyone's love. I'm a horrible person. I really am. The problem is, I don't know how to change," she continues.

I can't make sense of her rambling. "We can always change, Ryah. Who we are is a result of decisions we make daily. It's never too late to change," I offer.

"I appreciate the gesture, Kasey. I really do. But you don't understand. I'm a horrible, horrible person. I've done so many despicable things. That's who I am. I can't help it. I can't love."

"Ryah, why are you saying these things?"

"Because they're true. Come on. You've been around me. Can you honestly say I'm someone who deserves respect? Can you say that I deserve to be loved?"

"Everyone deserves to be loved."

"Not me," she declares. She's not crying any longer. Instead, her voice sounds spiteful.

"What happened?" I ask.

"It's no use."

"Ryah, stop it! I wouldn't have driven here if you didn't matter to me. For God's sake, I move in a few hours and I'm here because *you* matter. I'm here because I care," I shout. "So tell me why you're so upset. Please!"

"You're moving?" she asks.

"Yes. I'm moving to Chicago tomorrow," I answer. "Or today. I don't know. What time is it now?"

Ryah pauses. "Great. The last person in this world who can actually tolerate the sight of me is leaving."

"Ryah, I'm moving. We can still be friends," I assure her.

"I understand," she says in a solemn tone. She looks straight ahead without blinking. She is considering something, but I don't know what.

"Talk to me, Ryah. What happened?" Just then I hear a knock on the door. I look at Ryah to see if she's expecting someone. She looks confused too. "Who is that?"

"I have no idea. Should I answer it?" she asks.

"I don't know. You're not expecting anybody?"

"No. Oh, Jesus, hopefully it's not Steve," she says.

"Who is Steve?"

"Never mind," she says as she stands and walks to the front door. When she opens it, I see a tall man with blond curly hair.

"Bo!" Ryah exclaims. "What are you doing here?"

"Where is he? Is that him?" he asks in a hostile voice. I stand.

"Do I know you?" I ask him.

"Shut the fuck up. You're Kasey, right?" he yells as he pushes his way past Ryah.

"Bo, stop it. What are you doing?" Ryah shouts.

"I'm Kasey. What's the problem?"

He walks right up to me until his face is inches from mine. "What's the problem? You're the fucking problem. I hear you've been talking shit about me. Well, what do you have to say now, little man? Still think you can talk about fucking Ryah behind my back?" He's staring at me with such intensity that I take a step back to create some separation between us.

"I think there's been some sort of misunderstanding," I say as Ryah tries to step between us. She puts her hands on his chest. He swats them away.

"There's no misunderstanding. You didn't think I would find out about what you have been saying, did you? Well, I did. And now I'm here."

"Bo!" Ryah cries before she starts sobbing again.

"Stay out of this, Ryah," he commands. "If you weren't such a goddamn slut, I wouldn't be here. This pussy has been saying how he's fucking you behind my back. Aren't you going to say something before I make you eat your words?"

I look at Ryah and then back to Bo. "I never said any of that," I announce. "I don't know who told you those things, but they're wrong." That's when I see something in his hand. I hear Ryah scream as he raises his arm. Then—

CHAPTER FIFTY-FOUR
Have You Heard?

Elijah Noor

S carlett is hysterical. She tries to speak, but all I can hear are unintelligible sounds punctuated by heavy sobs.

"Where are you?" I ask as I motion with my hand for Phil to hurry over to the bar.

"I'm...I'm..." she mutters.

"Calm down. Where are you?"

"I'm at home," she utters before the sobbing becomes uncontrollable again.

"I'll be right there," I tell her. I hang up and tell Phil he will have to cover the bar because I have an emergency. I grab my blazer and rush out of Wayside.

I arrive at Scarlett's not knowing what to expect. She opens the door before I can knock and I see her red eyes. She takes one look at me and starts crying again.

"What's wrong?" I ask as I close the door behind me. She doesn't answer. She paces as she attempts unsuccessfully to catch her breath. I notice that her body is trembling. While I watch Scarlett's body shake involuntarily, I recognize the fleeting emotion I am experiencing as genuine concern for someone other than myself. It terrifies me.

"You...haven't you...heard?" she asks between gasps.

I'm confused. "Heard what?" I respond.

"Kasey...Bo..." she answers before her frenzied crying continues.

I grab Scarlett's arms to stop her from pacing. She can't look me in the eyes at first, and when she finally does, I have to look away. "What is it?" I beg. "Answer me!"

"Bo...Bo attacked Kasey." I can feel her arms shaking. Her body becomes limp. I help her sit in a chair so that she doesn't fall to the floor. She collapses into the chair and covers her face with her hands. I stand over her.

"What do you mean, Bo attacked Kasey? Why would he do such a thing?"

"I...I don't know," she manages to say.

"How bad is it?" I ask, still standing over her. She's sobbing. "Scarlett," I shout, "how bad is it?"

She looks up at me. Her hands fall to her sides. I've never seen anyone this distraught. "Kasey is in the hospital. I heard it's pretty serious. He might be in a coma. God, I don't know. I can't even think. Why would Bo do this?"

"What about Bo? Where is he?" I ask, trying to piece together the happenings from Scarlett's fragmented answers.

"He was arrested. I guess he's at the jail. I don't know what's going on. Why is this happening? I don't know what to do, Eli. I don't know what to do!" She screams the last part as she cradles her knees against her chest. She starts rocking in the chair.

I decide that Scarlett is too emotional to accompany me to the hospital. "Scarlett..." She doesn't even look up. She continues rocking in the chair while cradling her legs. "Scarlett, listen to me." She looks up at me. "You have to listen to me, OK?"

"I don't know what to do, Eli. I don't understand any of this. Why is this happening?" she repeats.

"Scarlett, you need to calm down and listen to me. I'm going to go to the hospital to check on Kasey's condition. I want you to stay here and wait for me to call. Can you do that? Will you be OK?" Scarlett grabs my hand. She squeezes it with all her strength.

"Don't leave me here by myself. I'm scared."

"Scarlett, I have to check on Kasey. I need you to stay here." She tries to pull me closer to her. I don't allow her to.

"Please don't leave me here. I can't be alone right now," she pleads.

"You have to stay here and wait for me to call. Can you do that? I have to check on Kasey." She lets go of my hand and stops rocking in the chair.

"What about Bo?" she asks.

"What about him?"

"I need to know if he's OK. I need to see him."

"I don't think that's a good idea right now."

"Why not?" Her bottom lip quivers when she asks the question.

"Because he's been detained and we're going to have to wait before we can contact him. In the morning, we'll call and check to see if bail has been set. By then we'll know how severe this all is. You have to promise me you're going to stay here. I need to know you're safe. I'll call you from the hospital as soon as I know something, OK?"

She starts rocking herself back and forth again. She looks defeated in every way. "OK. I'll stay here."

"Thank you. I have to know you're safe. I'll call you as soon as I know something. Trust me. Everything will be OK."

She looks up at me, almost in a trance now. "How do you know that?"

I've never seen Scarlett look so fragile.

CHAPTER FIFTY-FIVE
Waiting Room

Franki Rose

I rush into the hospital and demand to see Kasey. The woman at the desk says that he's not allowed any visitors because he is in critical condition.

"I need to see him!" I scream. "He needs me."

"Ma'am," the unmoved woman in scrubs begins, "I'm going to have to ask you to have a seat and wait until the doctors approve visitors. I will tell you that based on his condition when he arrived, they are unlikely to allow visitors for quite some time."

"What do you mean? What's wrong with him?"

"He's suffered head trauma. Right now, he's unresponsive. That's why he is considered critical."

"Oh my God! Will he make it? He has to make it. Please, tell me…"

The woman's impersonal expression cracks a bit. "He's in a coma. The doctors are doing everything they can to treat him," she says in a more compassionate tone. I can't move. My body feels heavy. "Ma'am, are you OK? Ma'am?"

When I wake up, I'm sitting in a chair with what appears to be a nurse as well as the woman from behind the desk both standing over me. They look worried.

"Ma'am? Can you hear me?" the nurse asks.

"What happened?"

"You fainted," the woman from behind the desk says. "You're getting your color back. Do you feel better?" The nurse is checking my pulse. I can smell her perfume.

"I think so." I am mortified. Everything feels like a dream.

"You're going to be fine," the nurse reports to me. "Here, sip this and stay seated for ten minutes or so," she directs as she hands me a plastic cup filled with cold water. I take a sip.

"Thank you."

"You need to stay seated for at least ten minutes. I need to go for now." The nurse turns to the woman and says, "Let me know if her condition worsens." The woman nods.

"Are you sure you're going to be OK?" the woman from behind the desk asks again. I think she feels bad that I lost consciousness.

"Yes. I'll be fine. I'm sorry. I'm embarrassed."

"Oh, nonsense. You're stressed out, that's all. You're not the first person to faint by my desk," she says while smiling. I smile too. I'm glad she's so understanding. As she turns to walk back to the front desk, I hear a door open.

Eli notices me right away. I must look terrible, because he does a double take.

"Franki, what happened to you?" he asks.

"I passed out," I reply.

"Jesus, what is going on? Are you OK?"

"I'll be fine." I take a drink of water. It's nice to see Eli. I feel calmer. "Are you here to check on Kasey?" I ask.

"Yes. Have you heard how he is?"

"They won't let me see him. He's in critical condition."

"Damn. Bo must have lost it."

"I don't understand. Does Bo know him?"

"I don't know. It's complicated," he says while looking away from me.

"What do you mean?"

"They were both seeing Ryah."

"What?" I can't believe what I'm hearing. *What is wrong with Ryah?* I always suspected something like this might happen. She is so careless with men. She forgets that just because she doesn't develop attachments to men, that doesn't necessarily mean that the men in her life don't become attached.

"I guess Bo freaked out and attacked Kasey. I'm not sure of the details. I guess Bo is in jail."

"I would hope so. He nearly killed Kasey."

Eli's expression is blank. "Let's hope Kasey pulls through," he relays in a solemn tone.

"I can't think about this. It's too much. Kasey will make it. He's tough. It's all so heartbreaking. He had plans to move to Chicago."

"What? Are you serious? Why?" Eli looks down at me again. His eyes study mine.

"He wanted a fresh start. He said he couldn't live in this town any longer. I guess now we know why."

"Our sins aren't forgiven that easily," Eli offers in a somber tone.

"I suppose not," I respond, not knowing what he means exactly. Eli sits down beside me. I look at him. I want so badly for him to hug me. He doesn't.

"I'm surprised you came here," Eli says after a brief silence.

"Why do you say that?"

"Because I thought you and Kasey—"

I cut him off. "There's nothing between us. We're friends. I'll always care about him. That's all," I assert while looking at Eli. Eli's expression lacks any visible emotion.

"That's not what I meant," he says. "I know you've moved on."

"What do you mean then?"

"Nothing. Forget it. It's not the right time to have this conversation." Eli turns his head and looks straight ahead at the television mounted on the wall.

"What conversation? What are you talking about? Please tell me."

"We'll talk about it some other time. We're here for Kasey."

I position myself in my chair so that I'm facing Eli. He doesn't turn his head. "Eli, look at me. Why won't you tell me what you meant?"

"It's not important," Eli says while still looking at the television.

"It's important to me. What conversation do we need to have?"

Eli maintains his stoic stare.

"Look at me, please," I plead as I touch his arm with my hand.

Eli turns his head and looks at me. He looks older, like he hasn't had a good night's sleep in a while.

"What do we need to discuss?"

"John," he says in a flat voice.

My heart races. I can feel my pulse throbbing in my neck. "John?" My voice cracks when I ask. I put the plastic cup to my lips and drink the rest of the water.

"Yes, John. Don't play stupid, Franki. I know you went on a date with some guy named John. I know about everything," he says. Eli then looks away and continues watching the television. *How can he be so cold?*

"I didn't go on a date. I met him to hang out as friends. That's all. Would you calm down? I wouldn't—"

"Don't do this, Franki," Eli interrupts. "It's not who you are. You're not a liar. It's unbecoming."

"Eli, I swear to you, it was nothing. I want to be with you. You're the one I care about."

"This is not what either of us needs," he says with such detachment that I almost cry immediately.

"Please, Eli. Don't do this to me," I plead.

"Do what?"

"Do this. I need you. What we have is real."

"Is what you had with John real too? What is real, Franki? Can you tell me? Do you even know?"

"Please, Eli."

"I can't deal with this right now. I need to make a phone call." Eli stands from his chair.

Instinctively I grab his arm.

"Franki, let go," he commands.

"Please. Don't do this. Don't leave me."

"You did it to yourself, Franki. You went on a date with John, and now you want to lie to me and claim that the day you spent with him didn't mean anything? How stupid do you think I am? Do you think you can tell me half truths and I'll believe them? The only one you're deceiving is yourself. Now, let go of my arm."

I feel weak. I let go of his arm. Eli glares at me as he stands over me. There's no compassion in his eyes. Everything stops. I can't breathe. I try to speak, but I can't. I wish he would cuss at me or belittle me. I want him to react. He doesn't. He takes one last look at me, and then he walks away.

CHAPTER FIFTY-SIX
Many Truths

Ryah Klein

I'm all alone. Kasey is in the hospital, and I can't get any of the staff there to tell me how he's doing over the phone. Franki won't answer my calls. Bo is in jail. I'm going crazy at home and no one cares. I don't ever want to see Bo again. I never thought he would do such a thing. Kasey's blood is still on my floor. I can't bring myself to wipe it up. I just keep looking at it. I've never seen such violence in real life. Kasey's complexion turned white after the second blow, and then he lost consciousness. All I could do was cry, but Bo wouldn't stop. No matter how loud I screamed, he wouldn't stop.

I go to my bathroom and open the medicine cabinet. I take out a bottle of prescription painkillers. I haven't taken one in a long while, but I can't stop shaking. I put two pills in my mouth and close the medicine cabinet. I turn on the faucet and cup my hands together. I hold my hands under the faucet until they fill with water. I lower myself and drink the water pooled in my hands. I tilt my head back and swallow the pills. It won't be long until I can't feel anything. It's sad that I crave numbness so often.

I sit at the kitchen table and drink a tumbler full of white wine. I feel a rush of exhilaration from the pills. I sip my wine as my body melts into the seat. My head feels heavy. I rub my face, and then I scratch my ear.

My eyes are dry. I want someone to talk to, but I have nothing to say. I take another drink of wine and sink in my seat until my head rests on the back of the chair. I'm almost asleep when I hear a knock on my door. I sit up. *Who can it be?*

I open the door to find Franki. I invite her in. She walks right past me without a greeting. She immediately paces back and forth in my living room. I'm too sedated to disguise my intoxication. My head wobbles when I walk into the living room. I sit down in a chair with hopes that Franki won't notice I'm fucked up.

"Where have you been?" She sounds angry.

"What do you mean? I've been here." It's becoming difficult to keep my eyes open.

"Did you even consider coming to the hospital to visit Kasey? What the hell is wrong with you?" Franki's hands are extended in my direction as if she's begging me to answer.

"I wanted to," I begin without finishing. I don't know what she wants me to say.

"But you didn't. I can't believe you. Eli told me everything. How could you sleep with Bo and Kasey and think that it wouldn't lead to something like this? Or do you even care? Are you that selfish? Kasey is in a coma. He might die. Doesn't that mean anything to you? Do you care about anyone besides yourself? This isn't a game, Ryah. People are getting seriously hurt. Is your pleasure really worth all this pain?" Franki yells.

She's never yelled at me before. I look away. My eyes fill with tears.

"Don't...don't you fucking dare start crying," she demands.

It's too late. Tears escape and roll down my cheeks. I look at her. She's not the least bit moved.

"Don't hate me," I beg.

"Just tell me you care. Tell me you never meant for this to happen. Give me a reason not to give up on you entirely. Please. I need a reason, because I don't know what to think anymore."

"Why do you say that?"

"I know you told Eli about John. You're the only person I told. I don't know why you did that, but it hurts me. It hurts me more than you'll ever know."

"I'm sorry." I can't catch my breath.

"Don't say you're sorry. I'm so sick of people saying they're sorry. Sorry doesn't make what has actually happened any less real."

I wipe the tears from my eyes. "What do you want me to do?"

"I want you to tell me the truth."

"About what?"

"Everything. Aren't we supposed to be friends?"

"We are friends."

"Then tell me the truth. You slept with Kasey while he was dating me, didn't you?"

"Franki—"

She interrupts me. "Just answer the question!"

The tears keep coming. My mouth is so dry I feel like I'm choking. "Franki, please. Not now."

"You're a fucking whore. You know that, right? I can't even look at you." Franki turns from me and walks toward the door. I attempt to stand, but instead my knees buckle.

"You don't understand," I yell between sobs.

"What don't I understand?" Franki asks as she turns around to face me. I want everything to stop so I can catch my breath.

"I wasn't always this way."

Franki sighs. "Don't make excuses, Ryah. Just don't. I can't listen to that right now."

I try to stop crying, but I can't. "Leave. Everyone else does. You shouldn't love me. No one should. I deserve to be alone."

"I don't know what to say, Ryah." Franki's disgust with me is obvious.

I look up at her and realize this might be the last time I ever see Franki. "There's something else," I begin.

Franki's glare softens. "What? What else could there possibly be?" she asks.

"Franki, I need to tell you something, because I know this may be the last time you ever visit me." I try to open my eyes but they fall shut again. "I hope that's not the case, but I understand if it is." She hasn't left yet. "I took your friendship for granted, and I...I'll never forgive myself for that. But I have to tell you this. I must," I inhale, willing the world to settle down, "be completely honest with you if there's any hope of you ever forgiving me."

"Spare me the dramatics, Ryah. What is it?"

I take a deep breath. "It's about Eli."

I can see the hatred in Franki's eyes. "What about Eli?"

"There's no easy way to say this."

"Ryah, say it now, or I'm never going to speak to you again," she commands.

"I slept with him," I confess. Franki doesn't respond immediately. "I'm sorry. I mean, he made me believe he cared about me, but I know now that he doesn't. I don't know how I could have been so stupid. I guess I wanted to believe a man could really love me."

Franki still doesn't respond. She's looking in my direction as if I'm no longer there.

"Franki, you're the only person who actually loved me. I know that now."

Franki doesn't speak.

"Can you ever forgive me?"

She doesn't answer me.

"Franki?"

CHAPTER FIFTY-SEVEN
Everything That Wasn't

Elijah Noor

Ryah is the last person I want to visit, but I'm worried. I think Franki may do something desperate. About an hour ago, Franki left a vague voice mail about her not being able to take it any longer. She repeated that sentiment twice, and then there was a long silence before she finally hung up. With everything that is going on, Ryah might be the last person Franki actually trusts. I park my car outside Ryah's apartment building and turn the engine off. I hope Ryah realizes I have nothing to offer her—or anyone else, for that matter. I have no excuses that might in some way explain everything that has happened. I can't control other people. I can only control myself. My motivation is fairly simple. I do what I do because I want to.

"What are you doing here?" Ryah asks as soon as she opens the door.

"Calm down," I say. "I wouldn't be here if this wasn't important."

"What is it?" Ryah demands as she stands in the doorway, blocking my entry.

"Can I come inside? It's about Franki," I reveal. Ryah's resolve softens when I say Franki's name. She steps aside and motions me into her apartment with her hand. She shuts the door and looks directly at me. Her fierceness has dissipated. She stands before me as the same tragic girl I have visited countless times in the past. Nothing has changed. All it would take is a single touch, and she would be mine. It's sad, really.

"So what is it?" she asks in a defiant tone.

"It's Franki. Have you talked to her recently?"

"Yes. Why, what's wrong?"

"I don't know. I was hoping you would know something. She called and left a depressing voice mail about her not being able to take it any longer. I have no idea what she means, and she's not answering her phone."

Ryah gasps. "Oh no," she utters under her breath.

"What? What's wrong?"

The color drains from Ryah's face. She sits down in a chair. Her eyes are fixed and unblinking.

"Tell me what's going on," I demand.

"I told her," Ryah says in a defeated voice.

"What did you tell her?"

"Everything."

"What does that even mean? Why are you acting this way?"

"I told her about us." Ryah appears completely disconnected from what she's saying.

"You did *what*? Are you crazy?" I shout. I can't believe what I'm hearing. I never thought Ryah was capable of such a selfless act.

"I had to. She already knew. She knew everything. I had no choice but to be honest with her if I want any chance of our friendship surviving. I betrayed her, and I'm supposed to be her best friend." Ryah looks up at me. "I need someone who cares about me, Eli. I'm not like you."

"What is that supposed to mean?" I look down at Ryah.

"You don't need other people. I understand that now. That makes it easy for you to discard people when you're finished with them. You only care about yourself. That's just who you are. But I'm not like you. I don't care about myself. That's why I need at least one person in my life that cares about me. It's all I have. Don't you understand that?" Ryah's eyes are glassy. I don't want to be here any longer.

"Listen, you need to go over to her place and see if she's OK. She won't talk to me, especially now. You're the only one she might respond to."

"It's too late. She doesn't care about me any longer. No one does."

"Stop feeling sorry for yourself. Franki is your friend, and she needs you. You have to check on her. If she does something to herself, you'll never forgive yourself." I turn from Ryah and walk toward the door.

"Eli," Ryah says from the living room.

I pause and turn around. "Yes?"

"Will you come with me? I can't be alone right now. Please, just come with me. If you ever cared about me, please, come with me. I don't know what I'll do if—"

"You'll be fine," I tell Ryah. "You don't need me." Tears fall from Ryah's eyes and roll down her cheeks. If I didn't know her, I might be moved.

Ryah sniffs. "I miss you, Eli. I know that's not what you want to hear, but I do. I don't know if that will ever go away. Part of me hopes it does."

"It will get easier. Emotions weaken gradually, until one day you realize you no longer feel anything at all."

CHAPTER FIFTY-EIGHT
Easily Broken

Franki Rose

The issues are too complex to unravel, so I decide not to try any longer. I draw a warm bath and light some candles I've placed along the edge of the tub. I ease into the water and feel my skin develop goose bumps in response to the warmth. I keep the hot water on just enough that it trickles from the faucet so the bath stays warm. I lean back until every part of my body is submerged except for my neck and head. I take a deep breath and exhale slowly. I rest the back of my head against the ceramic tub and enjoy the stillness.

While I soak in the tub, I think of everything I thought I had and how none of it was true. I keep rehearsing all the memories with Eli that I cherished so dearly. *I have to mean something to him, don't I?* He couldn't have faked all of those moments. *Were any of his smiles genuine? Is authenticity possible any longer?* When I close my eyes, I see Eli with Ryah. I envision her seducing him and pleasing him in ways that I couldn't. I want to hate her. I really do. She's such a slut. She lied to me about Kasey. Even then, she knew I really cared for Eli, yet she couldn't resist. Desire always was her priority. And now she doesn't have anyone who truly cares about her. I want to hate her, but I can't. *How can I hate someone who already hates herself?*

I lean over each candle on the edge of the tub and extinguish the flame with a gentle puff of breath. I lift the towel from the floor where I placed it and unfold it. I stand and wrap the cotton towel around me. I look down as the moisture on my body causes the towel to conform to my figure. I never liked my thighs. They look way too big for my body. I step out of the tub and wrap the towel I placed on the edge of the sink around my hair. I look at myself in the mirror. I don't look nearly as damaged as I feel. I look like I would any other evening after a bath. Sometimes pain isn't visible, even to the person experiencing it.

I considered how I would do it a long time ago. There are so many ways. It's difficult to decide. I didn't actually think it would ever progress beyond the fantasy stage. I suppose nobody thinks they will actually do it. That's what makes the thoughts easier and easier to accept. But it's the only option now. All I know is that I don't want to feel pain any longer. I want to experience the peace that has eluded me thus far. I feel relieved that it's almost over.

I never believed in taking medication. I didn't even take the pain pills I was prescribed after my wisdom teeth were removed. I saved the whole bottle, even though Ryah begged me for them. I told her that they made me sick and I threw them away. I don't know why I told her that. At the time, I thought I did so to save Ryah from abusing them. Now I suspect that on some level I wanted to save those pills for another reason. I spent so much time trying to protect everyone around me that I forgot to protect myself. Sometimes it's hard to know when someone needs help.

I turn off all the lights in my bedroom and light two tall candles stationed on my nightstand. I open the window so I can feel the cool October wind against my skin. I walk to the kitchen and fill a glass with cold water. I walk back to the bedroom. I look at the orange pill bottle and take a deep breath. *I won't feel anything*, I keep thinking to myself. I sit on the edge of the bed and place the glass of water on the nightstand. I open the bottle of pills and pour all the white tablets into the palm of my hand. I take another deep breath and in one motion push all the pills into my mouth. I bite down on them. They feel chalky against my tongue and have a bitter taste. I keep chewing until my mouth feels pasty, and then I lift the glass of water and drink until the glass is empty. I can't help but cringe from the aftertaste. I place the glass back on the night table and lie down. I feel dizzy. I turn my head and watch the flames from the candles flicker in the wind as puffs of black smoke snake slowly toward the ceiling. I thought I might experience some sort of grand revelation after I had taken the final steps, but there's nothing. My mind is blank. My body feels numb. I could easily mistake the euphoria that I feel for happiness, but I know that I'm not happy. It's a synthetic happiness that I feel. Maybe that's all there is. I watch the flame distort. Every puff of air from my open window causes the flame to grow. It's mesmerizing how it fights to remain lit. My eyelids are getting heavy. I want everyone to know how much I love them. I hope that when this is over my family and friends…

CHAPTER FIFTY-NINE
Is it Too Late?

Ryah Klein

I can see the light on inside the house, but Franki isn't answering the door. I knock with more force and wait. I press my ear against the door and listen for movement inside. I don't hear anything. I consider going home, but then I remember what Eli said. Franki needs me. I've let her down enough already. I can't do it again. This may be my last chance to show her that I care. I peer into the house through the living room window. I can see light coming from her bedroom. I know she's home. I'm scared. I take a deep breath and repeat to myself, "I can't let her down," as I walk around the house to her bedroom window. I find the window open. She's lying on her bed with two lit candles positioned on her nightstand. "Franki." I whisper so I don't startle her. "Franki, it's Ryah. Franki?"

My stomach drops and time stops when I realize Franki isn't asleep. I see a prescription bottle on the nightstand beside an empty glass. I climb in the window. Every movement I make is in slow motion. I watch myself frantically shake her. Her eyes remain shut. I start crying when I notice that her breathing is very shallow. "Franki!" I shriek. She doesn't look like herself. Her skin looks waxy. I dig into my pocket for my cell phone and dial 911. The operator answers. I don't know what I even say. I'm looking at Franki. I don't want to be the reason she doesn't wake up.

The ambulance arrives, the paramedics rush Franki away on a stretcher, and I'm left sitting on her bed crying. I have no one to call. I don't know what to do. I look over at Franki's nightstand and stare at the empty pill bottle. Wax drips down the sides of the candles. I cup my hand behind the top of each candle and blow until I extinguish the flame. I watch the smoke hang in the air and hope that this is not the last time I'm in Franki's house.

I arrive at the hospital, and as soon as I walk through the sliding automatic doors, I'm greeted by a gust of cold air that causes me to lose my breath. Everything smells sterile. Horrible paintings in cheap frames hang on the white walls. I shuffle to the reception desk and ask for Franki. They tell me to have a seat in the waiting room. Before I do so, I ask about Kasey. The receptionist tells me his condition hasn't improved from critical. I thank her and walk to the waiting area. I stare at the television. An old sitcom is on, but I don't remember its name. Every time the studio audience erupts with artificial laughter, I shudder.

I want so badly for someone to hold me and tell me everything will be OK. I text Eli, and as soon as I push the send button, I regret it. I know he thinks I'm weak, and I know he finds that unattractive. I don't want to be weak. I want to be strong, but I don't know how. My entire life I've been pretending to be somebody I'm not. What really saddens me is the realization that I don't know who I am. I always think of myself in terms of how others view me, but now that no one is around, I feel like...

CHAPTER SIXTY
No Escape

Elijah Noor

I see Ryah as soon as I enter the hospital. I didn't bother to answer her when she texted me about Franki. I consider leaving, but then Ryah notices me and I can't. I walk to where she's seated. I can tell she's been crying. Every time I start to feel the least bit sorry for Ryah, I remember watching her leave Wayside with that guy, and the numbness returns.

"How is she?" I ask.

Ryah looks up at me. She's shaking. I think she feigns sadness as a way to gain control of people. "They don't know. I found her. She took pills. She wouldn't wake up, Eli. I shook her and yelled, but she wouldn't wake up. I think she may have stopped breathing."

I turn from Ryah so that she doesn't see my concern. "Why the hell would she do this?" I ask out of frustration. "What could possess some-one so beautiful to do this?" Ryah starts sobbing uncontrollably, which only intensifies my anger. "Stop it! Stop making this worse."

"It can't get any worse," she says as tears drip off her chin. "Don't you get it? We did this to her. All of us. We destroyed her."

"That's nonsense. Franki is sick. She must be. No healthy person would react this way." I prepare to leave when I hear the automatic doors open. I turn to see who it is. It's Scarlett. As soon as I see her, I remember that I was supposed to call her but never did. *Is she looking for me? Has she talked to Bo?*

When Scarlett sees me with Ryah, she freezes. I can tell it hurts her, but she tries her best to conceal it. She walks toward me. I abandon Ryah and walk to meet her.

"Let me explain," I say as I approach.

"Don't bother. How bad is it?" she asks.

"Bad. Kasey is still in a coma and Franki Rose is unconscious. I guess she took a whole bottle of pills. Ryah found her unresponsive. They don't know if she'll make it or not." Scarlett lifts her eyes to the ceiling as if she's trying to make sense of everything. "How are you?"

"Not well, Eli. Bo called and wants me to post his bail once it's set. He didn't even apologize or offer any explanation for why he attacked Kasey. He asked me if I had talked to you. I figured you were still here. Why didn't you call? None of this makes sense. I don't understand it. Do you?"

"No," I tell her. "Are you going to post his bail?"

"I don't know. I don't want to. He's not even sorry. I don't think I ever knew the real Bo. It's all so sad."

"I agree." An awkward silence follows as Scarlett looks around the waiting room casually. I know she's trying to determine why Ryah is watching me.

Scarlett sighs. "What are you going to do, Eli?"

"What do you mean?"

Scarlett looks at me as if to say I can't be serious. "I mean, what are you going to do about Wayside and your father's house?"

"I don't understand."

"I figured you would want to move away from this town after all of this. I mean, there's nothing keeping you here any longer, is there?" I can't tell if Scarlett is asking this because of genuine concern, or if she is hoping that the recent happenings will in some way bring us back together. I don't think I care either way.

"There's no place to go, you know? I mean, I can't run from myself. No matter where I go, I'll be the same."

Scarlett stares at me. Her mouth opens as if she's about to speak, but she doesn't. I look back at Ryah. She's glaring at both of us. It's over now. There's nothing left for me to say.

On the way home I think of everything that has happened in the last few months. The series of tragedies replay in my mind in one continuous stream. I can't believe I don't feel broken. While I drive, a monarch butterfly becomes visible just before it makes contact with the windshield as my car speeds forward. Its mangled body casts a stain on the glass. I drive on and park my car at the house that once belonged to my father. I still don't consider it my house. I turn the engine off and sit in the car, thinking of everything I have lost and how dwelling on it doesn't change anything. I don't know why I never cry. *When did I become so desensitized?* Before I go inside the house, I stare at the butterfly wings stuck to the windshield as they flap in the breeze.

www.ingramcontent.com/pod-product-compliance
Lightning Source LLC
Chambersburg PA
CBHW030132180626
46812CB00002B/660